Journey to Fire's Keep

—

Journey to Fire's Keep

The Return to the Temple, Book One

Grady L. Owens

To order additional copies of this book, contact:
Xlibris Corporation
1-888-795-4274
www.Xlibris.com
Orders@Xlibris.com
80838

Contents

Prologue...7

1. Stephen...9
2. Feuerschloss...14
3. Jackolope...21
4. Emerald Forest..26
5. Elemental..32
6. The Revered..38
7. The Poor Wet Starving Mongrel 45
8. Flight...49
9. Beachfront..56
10. Justin...64
11. Angelo's Introspection...69
12. John's Introspection...74
13. Justin's Introspection...77
14. Stephen's Introspection..82
15. Coterie...87
16. Mission...94
17. Colloquy...99
18. Skepticism...104
19. Inquisition..112
20. Hindrance...119
21. Attack..125

Epilogue..137

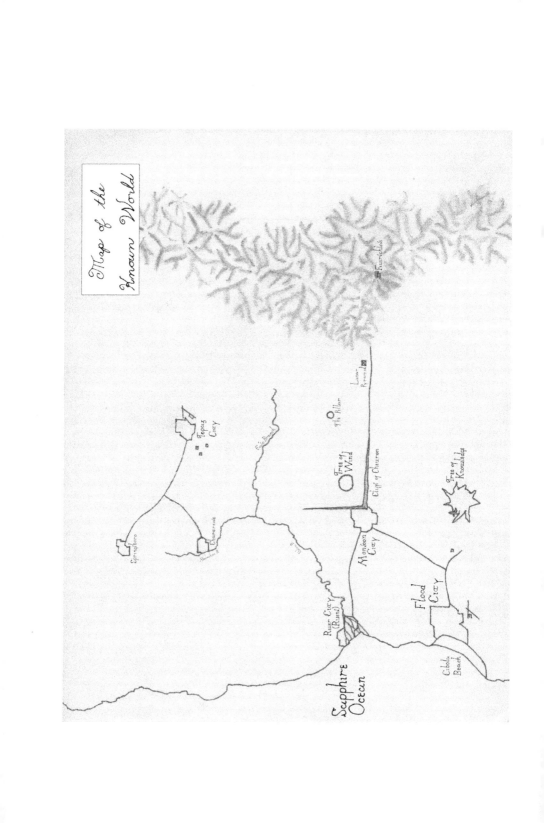

Map of the
Known World

Frenchies

Topaz City

Fir Forest

The Pillar

Springboro

Chancersville

Tree of Wind

Cliff of Chevron

Lunar Pyramid

River City
(Ruined)

Mandoon City

Tree of Knowledge

Flood City

Sapphire Ocean

Cibola Beach

Prologue

The presageful tempest streamed over the forest, coming to rest over a small crevice in the side of the hill. For the two cowering inside the hole, its paradoxical approach was simultaneously too fast and not fast enough; they had known this day would eventually come, yet they still chose to try to run. The woman, peering out the aperture for the silhouette that would confirm their worst fears, knew this had not been the wisest choice, but there was no other option in her perspective—she could not let *him* take her Firstborn.

In this moment, all the hard work they had done over the past several months to get to this place was coming to its true fruition—futility. As his outline came into view, she cried out in disbelief, anxious of what she knew was to come. Tears in her eyes, she turned to face her husband, his nervous back-and-forth pacing a constant contrast to the rain outside. "He's really coming! We've got to do something!"

"What can we do?" her husband inquired in an exasperated tone, stopping his frantic ambulation to turn and address her directly. "You know he's unstoppable. You knew this when we first started running from him! I don't even know why I agreed to—" The dialogue was abruptly halted by the rhythmic beating of wings. He had arrived. The baby, nestled in a crude cradle made of sticks, cried out in fear.

"Hide him!" the desperate mother roared. This time, he was not going to get what he came for. She was going to end this here.

The man, contrary to his initial demeanor, complied, swiftly hiding the child under a blanket, then covering it crudely with leaves. He next ran to hide himself, cowering behind a rock ledge leading deeper into the cave; he had not seen the figure in person and did not wish to change this, knowing full-well what he was capable of.

With a crack of thunder, the distinct image of a harbinger of destiny strolled confidently into the abode, head held high. The walls rattled as he yelled with a voice strong and loud, confident as the unrelenting downpour. "Where is it!?"

"What?" the mother asked, confident in her defiance.

"You, of anyone, should know," he said with an almost snakelike hiss. "*You* made the deal. Now is the time that I reap my share of the bargain."

"Never!"

"I let you live once, I won't make the same mistake again!" His voice escalated with every word. As he finished, a blast of fire leapt from his throat, engulfing and consuming the woman almost instantaneously. She collapsed in a pile of fine ash.

"How nice," he sneered. "The funeral pyre has already been taken care of." He found the child immediately, its wailing more than enough to reveal its whereabouts. *This face shall know me forever, and will know of his pathetically human father*, he thought. Perfect; the child would always submit. A demonic grin crept across his face, betraying his calm facade with a brief appearance of sheer sadistic rapture.

He turned and walked out the door as immediately as though nothing of consequence had happened there. The man, still cowering, waited until the beating stopped and the skies cleared. Only then, when he knew he was safe, did he mourn the death of his heroic, loving wife. He would never see her again.

Her soul, who had been watching the scene, also cried out in pain, in grief for her spouse. More than that, however, was the pain of unfinished business that she had to attend to—she had to see to it that her husband and child were happy.

1

Stephen

The morning arrived on schedule, sun inching above the horizon, shedding its first light on the sleepy town of Springsboro. The sound of chirping birds quietly permeated the atmosphere as the first few rays of sunlight filtered through the window into Stephen Doe's bedroom, silently playing with the prisms on the sill, throwing rainbows on the walls. Stephen didn't mind their presence, but his interest lay with the prisms.

The light wasn't what woke him up; a dull beating sound was sufficient for that. Stephen knew immediately who it was—Angelo Villalobos, his next door neighbor and best friend for many years. Every morning at around the same time, he would throw rocks at the window to get Stephen's attention. He wished the half-elf would learn how to knock on the door instead of threatening to break the window. He didn't want to have to pick up the broken glass shards out of the carpet; that wouldn't be fun.

Stephen was having the strangest dream before Angelo's persistence woke him up. What was it? All he remembered was a human killing an Orc with fire. He wondered what the meaning of this was until his contemplative trance was broken by his window doing the same thing; Angelo had thrown a rock that was much too big for the window to withhold. Stephen grabbed the gray stone and threw it back out the hole in the window, barely missing the young man below. The hint was clearly received, and he went to knock on the door.

Stephen rushed down the stairs, leapt over the polished wooden banister when he was close enough to the ground anyway that the impact wouldn't hurt his bare feet too much, and practically bounded across the floor to the front door. Pausing slightly to catch his breath after the sudden early-morning exertion, he turned the knob and pushed the door open. Sure enough, Angelo stood on the front porch, head tilted slightly. He had to have woken up fairly recently—his light-brown graying hair lay frizzed and disheveled between his ears. The stupid apologetic grin across his face did little to dispel Stephen's anger, though it did dull his response slightly.

"Why must you throw rocks at my window? You knew this was bound to happen. I tell you every time not to do it again, but you never heed my warning, and now, of all things, the window *does* break!"

The grin disappeared from Angelo's face. "I'm so sorry, Steve. I figure that you're a heavy sleeper, so you wouldn't hear me hit the door. So, I hit the window instead." The smile found its way back, followed by a slight nervous chuckle. Stephen's rage subsided.

"I'll have to fix that soon. But honestly, why do you do that? It should have gone out when we were kids!"

Angelo's expression changed from one of apology to one of confusion. "You mean we're not?"

Stephen almost smacked Angelo in the back of the head, but then remembered that he was, in fact, a half-elf—his kind could live much longer than humans, so the mentality of childhood must last longer for them as well. He shrugged half-acceptingly. "Whatever. Now, what do you want to do so badly that you had to wake me up by breaking my window?"

"I wanted to go hunting in the woods around the town." *So he* does *have a little adult in him.* "I just got a new longsword and wanted to try it out. You always bring good luck to my hunting ventures, so I was wondering if you wanted to come along."

"Uh, sure, just let me get some clothes on." He wasn't quite nude, but answering the front door in one's pinstriped boxers was not Stephen's idea of a grand start to the day; being asked to hunt in such a state was a tad unnerving. Besides, Angelo should have known by this point that Stephen preferred to wear his scaled armor during such ventures. He wasn't too fast, nor was he exactly well-built; sometimes it seemed like a miracle that he made it out alive. His armor had been the only thing that saved him from every attack up until now.

"Alright, I'll wait at the door."

Stephen went back upstairs to his room, being careful not to step near where the glass had fallen, and made his way to his chifforobe. The suit of armor lay at the bottom of the closet-like compartment, next to his shoes.

Its brown scales, taken from a southern monitor lizard, were fireproof; Stephen always liked how it shimmered in the sun. The suit itself flowed rather easily, and was almost silent during movement. It made for a perfect hunting tool, especially when allied to Angelo's mastery of swordsmanship. He pulled it out along with a pair of sturdy boots and placed the items carefully on his still-unkempt bed.

Hanging above these were varying shirts for varying occasions. Most of them were for lounging about, but there were a few fairly nice ones mixed in. He rarely wore these; however, being nice shirts, they hung with the others. Swiftly selecting a plain white t-shirt—to avoid pinching skin between rough scales, of course—he placed it on the bed beside the armor and closed the door. A simple pair of leather trousers would do for his lower half, so he pulled a pair out of one of the other drawers. Below this was his undergarments drawer, and still below was his sock drawer. Pulling one relevant article from each, he turned his attention to getting dressed. Normal morning hygiene, it seemed, would have to wait, as Angelo *was* waiting on him.

Having completely and properly clothed himself for the occasion, Stephen hurried back downstairs in the same manner as before, to the front door where Angelo was itching to get going.

*   *   *

"Diablo! Diablo! Where are you when I need you? Diablo!"

The summoned half-orc appeared at the door, clearly somewhat annoyed. "What do you want?"

"It's about time you returned!" Asmodeious hated waiting for anything. It made him crankier than usual, and he was always rather argumentative. "Did you find it?"

Diablo's disposition shifted from annoyed to nervous. "Umm . . . No . . . Not exactly . . ."

"*WHAT!* You didn't find it!?"

"Sir, I looked in a 50 kilometer radius of the keep! It's nowhere to be found!" Diablo tried to sound reassuring. "I'm sure if you just let another one grow in its place—"

"I'm not worried about how I look in the mirror, you damned fool!" Asmodeious bellowed. "That was an extremely valuable object with unspeakable magical properties! It was a limited resource!"

"Sir, I apologize for my shortsightedness—"

"You, of anyone, should know now important that was! You're one of the best sorcerers in the land!"

"Yes, of course—"

"Must I remind you—"

"No, sir, I know, my father—"

"NEVER INTERRUPT ME!"

Diablo was used to the yelling and the arguing by now. He *had* to get used to it; he had been raised by the monstrous Asmodeious Bruté for as long as he could remember. It had formed a sort of callousness to him. This was, of course, all according to the older mage's will; he desired a proper underling, one who would obey because of a similar mindset, instead of out of fear. The younger Diablo was almost there already—each day, he hated the world more and more. "I'll go looking again."

"No, you've bungled this up enough already. *I'll* go look for it."

"You? But sir, what if it's near a town? How will you explain—"

"If it's by a town, I'll also get some target practice in." He puffed an ember. "No one will know I was there."

Diablo, relieved that he didn't have to do any more work at least, shrugged and returned to his studies.

*   *   *

All was silent. The only movement detectable was that in the shadow cast by the windblown leaves of the trees. A large, fifteen-point buck stood before the duo in a slight clearing, grazing on the local foliage. Upwind, the two friends lay silently, motionless—the thrill of the hunt was upon them.

Angelo moved forward quickly while the deer grazed; it was oblivious to his position. As Angelo drew his weapon, the light stopped shining on the grass. The wind steadily grew in force, giving the deer enough incentive to look up; upon seeing the two others, it ran out of the thicket. Angelo, both disappointed at the loss of a hunt and being naturally curious, looked up as well. Large, ominous, dark clouds billowed overhead. Stephen, seeing Angelo's actions, mimicked them.

"Angelo, it was clear not five minutes ago, wasn't it?"

"I thought so too, but this storm . . ." Angelo suddenly felt more like running than hunting. A strong gale spontaneously surged through the wood and a dark shadow fell on the ground. A huge form flew by as lightning lit up the sky, providing a stark outline of something quite monstrous. Neither Stephen nor Angelo could tell what it was, but they knew it could probably kill them if it wanted to. The storm lasted for about an hour, during which the duo cowered beneath a hollow tree.

2

Feuerschloss

The mountain range jutting against the sky to the East was omnipresent; everywhere in the known world, their profile was visible. It was for this reason they were never given a proper name; if someone were to mention "the mountains", everyone listening in would know exactly what mountains were being referred to. They were a formidable barrier, to be sure; however, it was just that challenge that pushed mankind to explore them. Passes were designated early in the history of civilization, and indeed even a few cities sprang up amongst the jagged peaks, clinging to the very rock like a lichen, every bit as sensitive. Those who resided in this forced near-solitude referred to themselves as Grecians, and were known as one of the most peaceful groups of people ever to have lived.

One mountain, however, was avoided by most. Steeper than other peaks was this rise, its top a bellowing crater of brimstone—it was dubbed Fire Mountain by those who first encountered it. A volcano of monstrous proportions, it nestled near the Amber Forest on the very Western edge of the range, spewing clouds of ash and soot. Until the invention of the airplane, those who strayed near Fire Mountain willingly were deemed insane and assumed dead upon set-out; such events were even treated as funerals to assist those who would indeed be grieving the loss of their loved ones.

The first pilots to cross the mountains near this ominous peak, upon returning regaled stories in local taverns about a wholly unbelievable sight—a castle, perched upon the very rim of the caldera. Walls of purest satin black, it appeared as though the rock would not even reflect light; the structure towered over the steep slope to the West of the volcano, easily taller than most buildings anyone had ever seen. A spire rose from each of the castle's four corners, the pillars of stone seeming to rise from out of the ground as though from the center of the Earth, so sturdy was their foundation upon this hellhole of a mountain. Those who believed these tales bestowed the title of Feuerschloss to the legendary keep.

It was to this intimidating abode Asmodeious returned, a smile of pleased malevolence on his face and an item of immense concern in his grasp.

Diablo heard the loud creak of the castle doors opening. The deafening booms that followed could only mean one thing—Asmodeious had returned in a good mood. He must have found it. The booming footsteps turned into almost silent ones, confirming the younger mage's hopes—he would not be fried today. He returned to the handiwork before him. At the moment, he happened to be forging a ring encrusted with magic. It would allow the wearer to become invisible, enabling a superior surprise attack. When he finished, he heated it one last time in magma to seal the magic and set it on his talisman shelf to dry. He wasn't going to go see Asmodeious unless he called.

"Diablo!" The call occurred not five seconds after the thought; it brought with it a great disheartening. "Diablo! Come here this instant!"

He knew that to not be there as soon as he was called was a greater risk than what most insurance policies would willingly cover, so he ran out the door and yelled off the second floor walkway to his master in the great entry hall below. "Coming, sir!"

"Get down here, quickly!" Asmodeious' voice had a ring of ambition, of excitement, rather than anger and resentment. Diablo enjoyed that—it meant that the evil must be growing. He ran eagerly down the walkway, nearly stumbled down the massive gothic staircase, and hurried over to Asmodeious' position. The elder pulled something out of his black cloak. "Here it is."

Diablo gazed at the object with a confused astonishment. "Wow . . . it's so dull, but the feeling of magic overflows from within."

"Yes, so powerful, yet so indiscrete. That way it doesn't seem extraordinary to non-magical mortals."

Diablo whistled in admiration. "Can I have a piece? Magic that strong would be extremely useful in some of the stuff I'm working on!"

"No!" Asmodeious snapped. "I only get this chance about once a century. The magic is most potent when it's whole. Besides, I only get a limited amount."

Admittedly disappointed, Diablo gave a shrug of resignation. "That's understandable." His expression turned from letdown to curiosity. "So where did you end up finding it?"

Asmodeious paused as his mood flipped visibly. "Thank you, Diablo, for bringing up a sore subject. I had to triple your radius before I found this."

Diablo had to think about this a while; he wasn't very mathematically inclined. Any time his magic required any form of math, he usually gave up; there were very few instances in which he would continue, but most of these left him with a headache that, in his opinion, would kill a bull moose. "Add the zero, carry the one . . . 150 kilometers!? I don't remember you going that far when you lost it!"

"No, you don't remember me going out that far when I *screamed* at you about it. You weren't there when I lost it, so you wouldn't have been able to remember such an incident. Please don't lie to me using poor logic. You know it upsets me."

Diablo, unsure of what this "logic" was, ignored the jab and continued pondering. "Hey," he thought aloud, "isn't there a town about 150 kilom—"

"There *was* a town."

"Oh."

Diablo knew exactly what that meant. With no further questions, and the very good possibility that more would result in some sort of pain—he feared the agonizing kind, but it would more likely be excruciating, knowing his master—he went back upstairs to his lab. This left Asmodeious alone in the great hall. He just stood there for a while, remembering the town, all the people running, screaming . . . it made him feel all warm inside for some reason. He enjoyed that. Diablo heard the steps as Asmodeious left the foyer for one of his downstairs labs.

Feuerschloss was a rather large keep. Having been built straddling the edge of a volcanic crater, much effort had gone into supports on the side facing the large pool of molten rock. As a result, there had been much room on that particular side for the various additions Asmodeious required when he took over the facility. Seven different floors had been annexed in this manner, each serving a different purpose. The absolute bottom was Asmodeious' bedroom—there was very little else such a dangerous place was good for. Above this, in ascending order, were two laboratories for pet projects, a lab for possible commissions (these never came about, and the mage often wondered if he shouldn't use it as a broom closet), a floor entirely devoted to practicing various arts of weaponry, a library, and a laboratory specifically set aside for Asmodeious' most diabolical schemes. Asmodeious chose to work in the bottom-most lab, as that also happened to be the floor where he kept most of his other artifacts.

When his descent was finally complete, he placed the item on a shelf with the rest of his magical relics. Each one would come in handy later, but how, Asmodeious knew not. He collected them all the same; if nothing else he enjoyed looking at them, imagining the power they'd bring him, especially the new addition. He stared at it for a full half-hour.

Eventually, Asmodeious pulled himself away from his trophies and decided to practice some of his own magic. He proceeded to the Feuerschloss library of spell books, whereupon he decided to look for a spell book out of the hundreds that he hadn't used in a while, in order to get a little bit of a rotation in his routine.

He went to the section he had neglected for some time, in the very back of the library, and started leafing through the books at his eye level. As he read the titles aloud, he tossed them out onto the floor, knowing Diablo would pick them up later. "Prophesy, no . . . divining, no . . . alchemy—Alchemy!? Why do I still have this human quack magic book?" Then, another book caught his eye. He pulled it out.

This particular book was quite dusty, as books are wont to become after sitting on a shelf for hundreds of years. After Asmodeious blew it off carelessly and finished coughing, he read the label—*The Spellbook of Matter Transformation. Interesting*, he thought to himself. *This could be really fun.* He hurried back down to his lab to leaf through the procedures described in the book, unsure of what to do.

A few different concepts caught his eye. The Philosopher's Stone obviously intrigued him, as did the Monkey's Paw, but he had seen both in other books before. Besides, they were more like parlor tricks than true magic. Most two-bit magicians had at least attempted both, and many enjoyed marginal success; it really wasn't the sort of thing to truly test the master's mettle.

He came across a chapter on elementalism, which struck his fancy. "Aha! Here's what I'll do!" he exclaimed as he came across a rather interesting segment. "An Elemental Summoner: a talisman that gives one of the five Grecian elements, depending on the chanted incantation, life! Now, what will I need?" The list of ingredients was rather long, but Asmodeious was finding most of them rather well; he didn't keep a stockroom full of possibly useful materials just for show.

"Griffin feather . . . here they are! I only need one. Lava flow . . ." He rolled his eyes. "As if we could possibly have a shortage of that stuff. Here we go . . . Jackolope antler . . ." He pulled out an empty jar with the appropriate label. "Crap! Where am I going to get one of those at this hour?" He thought briefly to himself. "I guess I'm going to have to get one myself. Jackolope aren't all that hard to find around here. I'll stock up." He moved towards the front door. As he entered the main hall, he shouted for his apprentice. "Diablo!"

"Yes, sir?" Diablo came out of his lab a little faster than last time. Asmodeious liked that; punctuality was important for underlings to understand and practice. He looked up at Diablo, still standing on the second floor balcony. "I'm going out to gather some supplies. Guard the Feuerschloss, but don't get too behind on your work. I shouldn't be too long."

"Naturally. As you wish, master." Diablo had to shout, as the first floor was almost thirty feet below. They both went through their respective doors simultaneously.

*   *   *

Angelo and Stephen remained shivering inside the tree until they were sure all danger had passed. When the coast was obviously clear and the rain had ceased, they cautiously crept out. Angelo was the first to break the silence. "What was that?"

Stephen gazed up at the sky, still slightly overcast. "How should I know?"

Angelo shrugged. "Well, I didn't know, and I figured you might—"

"It was a turn of phrase. And stop figuring! It gets you into too much trouble, and I usually end up with the consequences!"

"Sorry." Angelo allowed for a slight pause. "*Do* you have any idea—"

"No!"

"None at all?"

"None whatsoever!" Stephen sighed. "Let's go home; I don't feel like hunting anymore, thinking that there's something out there possibly hunting us."

"Yeah, me neither."

The two surely soiled friends started toward the town that they had lived in for all their lives. As they approached, an odd smell filled their nostrils; it was faintly familiar, reminding Stephen of summer days, when he and his brother would chase each other in the yard while his father worked the grill, a meal in preparation. Something was wrong with the atmosphere; Angelo couldn't quite figure it out, but the sound was different in a subtle manner. It made both of them uneasy.

When the pair finally returned, a startling sight met their eyes—the town was gone. In its place was what appeared to be a fine black powder.

"Where'd the town go?" Angelo whispered, frightened, eyes wide and quivering. Stephen had already put two and two together, but as it was obvious his companion had not, he said nothing. He just shook his head in astonishment. He tried to hold back his tears, but he couldn't; the strain was causing his lower lip to tremble.

"Oh my god . . ." had Stephen been looking at Angelo, he would have certainly seen a small glass globe with a wire filament in it appear above his head, then light up. There was no holding back the torrent any longer. "NO!"

The town had indeed been burned to the ground. Not a single house remained standing, and it appeared as though no one was left alive. Just to be sure, Angelo ran as fast as he could to the place of his childhood, kicking up the ashes of others along the way. Once there, he found two charred, blackened skeletal figures, flesh seared to the bone—his mother and father. Wailing in absolute anguish, Angelo embraced their now crumbling bodies one last time, his tears carving channels in their charcoal faces. The people who had raised him . . . *how could someone be so heartless?* he wondered to himself.

"Stephen, what could do such a thing?" Angelo asked between gasps for air.

"I'm not sure," he replied, "but it looks intentional." Stephen, whose parents had died years before, was not stricken by grief as hard as Angelo, but was still quite tearful. These were people he had known since he had been old enough to remember their faces, and now every single one of them was gone. Many of them were impossible to find, indistinguishable from the rest of the ash and cinder.

"I swear . . ." choked Angelo, "if it's the last thing I do, I will—" he gasped.

Stephen wasn't having the same difficulty breathing, but he shared Angelo's sentiment whole-heartedly. "I swear to avenge everyone. All of these people were completely innocent; what crimes could they have committed to deserve such judgment?" He lost composure again, in grief over the loss of the town, but also in fear of what he was sure they would have to face eventually.

"So," inquired Angelo, wiping moisture from his face with a sleeve, "what do we do now? Where do we go from here?"

Stephen looked up into the woods, in the direction the storm had appeared not minutes before. "Honestly, I don't know what we're going to do, but that storm . . . something didn't seem right about it." He didn't know why, but Stephen almost felt as though the storm was sentient, or perhaps controlled by something that was. He decided to keep this bit of information to himself, lest he upset Angelo any more. "Perhaps we should set off in the direction it came from; maybe we'll find something."

Angelo sniffed and nodded. "That makes sense, I guess." He gathered his composure and began marching purposefully into the woods again.

"Angelo, what are you doing? We need to prepare, and at the very least give the bodies we can identify a proper funeral! We can't set off just yet."

"Stephen, if there is a single body responsible for what has happened here, I want to destroy it as soon as possible! You were right; that storm was highly suspect; we both hid in fear from it! And what of that shadowed figure? If we set off now, maybe we'll have a chance of finding it and stopping it."

Stephen sighed, frustrated and understandably stressed; this had just become an all-around bad day. "Very well, we'll proceed now. The main road through Emerald Forest seems the best match to the storm's flight path."

And so it was agreed that the duo would set off on a quest to find what exactly had happened to their town, and to avenge those who were lost. They set off into the Emerald Forest together, Angelo's sword at the ready, eyes peeled for anything out-of-place.

In the rubble behind them, a single pane of glass lay, unbroken and unmended. Stranger still, nothing was there to have previously shattered it.

3

Jackolope

All was silent, except for the occasional roar from the volcano; the indigestion that it received from consuming the acidic molten rock wreaked regular havoc upon the heart of the mountain. The trees swayed in a breeze that always brought moisture from the ocean. Light rarely shone through this canopy of leaves, but it was enough for Asmodeious to see with his extraordinary eyesight. Many magical creatures lived in this forest; Asmodeious himself could remember his childhood here. He loved the power he lauded over all the creatures, and still did.

Ahead, a slight movement caught the mage's eye. He looked toward it. A unicorn had emerged in the small plot before him, having decided to graze. *We do have a paucity of unicorn horns and blood*, thought Asmodeious. He crept ever-so-slowly toward his prey, careful not to make a single sound. He morphed his left index finger into a long black talon. The unicorn made no indication that it had heard his approach. He waited . . . waited . . . then attacked.

Asmodeious sprang shrieking at the unicorn, his left arm outstretched. The creature, hearing its attacker's battle cry, spun to kick him. As its legs went out behind it, Asmodeious rolled over in midair and landed under the unicorn's stomach. The claw went straight up, through its chest. A massive struggle ensued. The unicorn, shocked at feeling such pain, began convulsing to try and get Asmodeious out from under it. The horn came dangerously close several times. Asmodeious, using his claw to its full advantage, slit the hide of the unicorn between its ribs. He then pulled out a flask and started collecting the blood flowing out of the open wounds.

After the flask was full ("Who would have thought the beast would have so much blood in it?"), Asmodeious stood up, brushed himself off and, backing up to view the complete scene, watched the creature die in agony and pain. He enjoyed it; it had been a good kill. Knowing that leaving such a large portion of meat was not only wasteful but downright helpful to the local wildlife, he took the body. *Now*, he thought, *to find a jackolope.*

In all the magical encyclopedias one will ever be able to find in the world, jackolopes have been listed as very secluded individuals who abhor social contact; Asmodeious, however, having grown up in their vicinity, knew better than all that—he knew they actually lived in villages. The ones that most see are guards, sentries making sure the villages aren't seen. Asmodeious could remember having killed one as a child and entering the tiny town. The panic that ensued was justified—no one had seen anything like him, not even the elders. He soon grew bored of seeing them running in frantic circles, so he left. The knowledge of this village would prove useful after all.

As he continued on his brief journey, he soon came upon the neck of the woods where the micropolis laid. Again, he killed one of the guards, but this time, he put the body in a sack he brought with him. He left the unicorn corpse before entering; it was starting to smell, which would definitely alert the rest of the town of his presence, emptying it before he could get his appendages on anything of any use at all. Asmodeious felt deja-vú as he watched the jackolopes scurry around. They were fairly easy to kill; the only effort put forth was bringing his hand down fast enough to crush their relatively fragile skulls. He collected five more, then went back for the unicorn. He revealed his hideous nature to the silent witnesses of the forest, alighted, and headed back to Feuerschloss.

*   *   *

Diablo, growing bored with the trinkets he had created, went to the library of spellbooks to find something new. He decided to go to the back, as he had seen most all the other books. The first thing to catch his attention was a small pile of books left haphazardly on the floor. He reasoned that they were probably the ones that Asmodeious had seen but not wanted to use—in other words, they were definitely up for grabs. Why else would perfectly good books just be left on the floor? He started flipping through them.

"Divining, no . . . Levitation, no . . . Alchemy—Alchemy!? Why does he still have this human quack magic book?" He was now at the bottom of the pile. "*Prophesy.* Hmm . . . I might actually be able to have fun with this."

Diablo took the book upstairs to his lab. There, he opened the book near the middle, chose a random page, and read the title aloud. "The Clairvoyance Cauldron, what you see in every witch movie. I suppose I could use something like that." Seeing no ingredient list, he decided to read through the procedure; if no ingredients were listed, it was usually a safe bet that the necessary incantation made mention of what was required. Confirming Diablo's knowledge on the subject, the first note read "Add the ingredients as you say the incantation and they come up." He read on, determined what ingredients he would need, and began gathering them up from various places within his small personal laboratory. Once everything was ready, he started the incantation and mixing. "Bubble, bubble, toil and trouble . . ."

When he finished, a rather large explosion rattled the contents of the room and shot smoke throughout. Then, as spontaneously as it had erupted, the smoke was sucked back into the cauldron. The lumpy, red surface of the mess that had gone in smoothed out and transmuted into a substance of a silvery luster. Diablo was reminded of liquid mercury in a bowl by its appearance. He glanced back at the book. It provided directions, such as setting security modes and working the built-in alarm clock. He wasn't very interested in the clock, but the security system sounded like a good idea. He could monitor anything within a certain radius of the cauldron, according to the manuscript.

Diablo touched the surface of the concoction in the cauldron as the book indicated. It shimmered, then displayed a menu with three options: security, alarm, and browse.

"Security," Diablo said.

The cauldron's surface shimmered again. A new menu appeared. The new choices were radius size, password, and power. Taking his cues from the pages beside him, he made the appropriate settings for what he wanted to accomplish.

"Power on. Radius size, ten miles. Password . . . ." He thought about this long and hard; a good password was crucial. He seemed to remember Asmodeious saying something about how a man's password was a key to his soul, so it should be unique, fitting, and utterly impossible to guess.

"Fire's Keep."

The surface shimmered again—it was set. Any movement within ten miles of the cauldron would be displayed. Currently, there was an aerial view of the lab, with Diablo and the cauldron in the center. In the upper right-hand corner, a dot on a map of the lay of the land for ten miles of Feuerschloss flashed, signalizing other movement at that point.

Diablo touched the map at the blip, and the scenery changed. Asmodeious was now framed within the confines of the bowl, flying toward the castle, a large bloodied bag in his hand. *He must have obtained what he went for*, Diablo thought. It also looked like today's evening meal was going to be bigger than usual. He knew his master would be returning soon, so he rushed down to the front entry to greet him, eager to show off his new toy.

*   *   *

Asmodeious could easily see Feuerschloss from where he was in the sky. He was going to sleep well tonight; the volcano was smoldering as if it were going to erupt. He would have to warn Diablo—even for being a half-orc, his skin was less resistant to molten rock. When he returned to Feuerschloss, Diablo was standing at the main gate, waiting for him. Perhaps standing is the wrong word—bouncing seemed more apt a description. "Asmodeious, I must show you something!"

"Can it wait? I've got our dinner here; I'd much rather eat it now so I can get the magical relics off of it. Besides, it will get cold otherwise."

Diablo inspected the damp brown sack curiously. "What is it?"

"A unicorn and a few jackolope."

"I never really had a taste for unicorn," explained the half-orc, shrugging, "but I suppose a jackolope steak would do just fine."

Asmodeious had no real complaints either way; in the end, he probably would have chosen the unicorn that evening anyway. The two ate their meal in the dining hall, opposite the great hall from Diablo's lab on the first floor. Diablo ate hurriedly; he wanted to go toy with his cauldron again. In spite of all his hurrying, however, the two finished at the same time. "Alright," began Asmodeious, "what is it you wanted to show me?"

They went up to Diablo's lab, wherein Diablo showed Asmodeious the cauldron. It wasn't quite amazement with which the elder admired the cauldron; it was something more along the lines of nostalgia.

"Wow, I haven't seen one of these in centuries! Let's see if I still remember how to work it." He touched the surface. It shimmered, then displayed "Password?"

"Oh, let me handle this," Diablo said, having already forgotten that he had put a password on it. "Fire's Keep."

"Creative, yet easy enough to remember that you won't have to write it down. I like it."

The security menu came up. Asmodeious saw the various choices, then got an idea. "Radius size, 150 miles."

"Uh, Asmodeious, is that such a good—"

"I know what I'm doing."

The little map exploded with various points of flashing light. One dot seemed isolated towards the northwestern edge. Asmodeious poked it.

A town was shown. Or, at least, what had clearly been a town at one point. The outlines of houses, streets, and shrubberies were easily visible, but everything there had been carbonized. Nothing remained standing. Diablo knew as soon as he laid eyes upon the setting that this was Asmodeious' doing, a thought confirmed by the master's explanation. "That's where I found it. Wait . . . what's this?"

There were now two dots blinking within the same proximity. One signified the town quite obviously, but what was the other? Asmodeious seemed almost unnerved as he prodded the new marker.

Two people, a human and a half-elf, were walking together down a dirt road that seemed to connect their location with the charred remains of the village. The human wore scaly armor, while the half-elf sported a longsword.

Diablo postulated on their actions. "Could they be on their way here from the town?"

Asmodeious was livid. "No one gets killed by Asmodeious and lives!"

"Why are you so upset?" inquired the apprentice. "They're just a couple of common people. They can't harm you."

"The half-elf can't; he looks oddly familiar. The human, though . . . I sense a form of magic in him stronger than mine." Asmodeious tapped his chin. "Luckily for me, he hasn't harnessed it yet, but there's no telling what may happen when they get here!"

"Don't worry, Asmodeious," muttered Diablo reassuringly. "They probably just happened upon that town and have nothing to do with it. I'm sure they're just out hunting." His expression implied he felt otherwise; dread that strong could not be kept hidden.

4

Emerald Forest

Asmodeious was highly disturbed by what he was seeing. He knew for a fact that he had decimated the town—how could anyone or anything have possibly lived through that? Unless, of course, they were like Asmodeious himself. This possibility upset him the most; any competition he had ever faced in the past had been rightly quelled, but none had survived like these two. There wasn't so much as a burn mark on either figure! The human . . . there was something truly unnerving about the power that seemed to flow over him. Could he have been the cause of their survival? There weren't many beings out there with a magic strong enough to repel his fire; this thought only made him more perturbed.

True, it had been a while since he had used a Clairvoyance Cauldron, but it didn't take years of use and an expertise on the subject to read the map in the corner of the display. While the region was not that familiar to him, he knew the surrounding woods by the name given to them by the Deltanians who first colonized the region many centuries ago—the Emerald Forest. He knew of only one major thoroughfare that traversed the woodland and connected to Springsboro; if they weren't traveling that road, they were at least near it, and thus would be easy enough to find. He made to leave when he caught a motion out of the corner of his eye. Rather, it was a lack of motion—the two people had ceased in their trek and now appeared to be arguing back and forth.

Asmodeious had seen and heard of Clairvoyance Cauldrons with sound features, but not only had he never used one, he wasn't sure if the one before him had such a trait. As much as it upset him, he knew his underling would probably know the answer. "Does this cauldron have sound capabilities?"

Diablo shrugged. "I think so. Let me see how to configure the auditory properties . . ." He began speed-reading through the pages describing the cauldron. "Ah, here we are. Sound on."

*   *   *

Stephen stopped in the middle of the road, looking about warily. "Angelo, I don't know about this forest. It's kind of, well, creepy."

Angelo was forced to stop and turn around. The comment had come out of nowhere, and didn't make any sense to him. The leaves above were thin enough to be translucent, providing a calm atmosphere of permeating green; the light refreshing breeze only enhanced this effect. Birds chirped from nowhere in particular, and even the faint scent of the previous rain made the atmosphere that much more pleasant. "How so, Stephen? It's Emerald Forest. This is one of the nicest, least creepy places anywhere!"

"I know; it's just that for the last five minutes or so, I've felt like somebody's been watching us. You know that feeling, don't you?"

Angelo shrugged. "I cannot say that I do. I've certainly not felt anything out-of-the-ordinary since we began."

Stephen was truly disconcerted by this forest. He didn't know why, but it gave him the creeps. It wasn't as if there was a reason for it; as Angelo had said, this was one of the greenest, nicest, least spooky places in the world. In spite of all the leaves and canopy, light was still plentiful. Desperate for any excuse to leave however, he quickly thought of what might be nearby. "Hey, don't we need supplies?"

"What kind of supplies were you thinking of?"

"It could take us weeks, even months to even find out where we're going. We'd need food, water—"

"We could hunt, and drink out of streams." Angelo could tell Stephen was just making up excuses at this point, but if Stephen could talk his way out of this, he was willing to play along.

Stephen floundered a bit. "Yes, well, what if there are no streams ahead? What if we run into a desert? We'd need backup supplies, shelter, a weapon for me . . ."

He had hit upon a good point—though there was little chance of coming across a desert, there was still the need for Stephen to carry a weapon of some kind. It just wasn't safe for him otherwise, no matter how lucky his armor might have been. But what was nearby? "Where did you have in mind to procure these 'necessities'?"

"Well, if my memory serves me correctly, there's a town down that way." Stephen pointed up ahead to a point where the trees and foliage seemed to split on the right side of the road. "My brother's a merchant there. He could probably get us stuff at a discount. I think the town's name is Chartreuse."

Angelo shrugged and nodded in agreement, a motion that looked odd on any humanoid but was as natural as sneezing to the young half-elf. "Okay then, let's go to Chartreuse."

The town was relatively nearby, just as Stephen had said, though it did take them most of the afternoon to get there from where they had stopped. It was a beautiful, quaint little village by a stream. Until they had arrived, Angelo was mildly confused by the name, but that changed upon a single glance. Everywhere they looked, the hue for which the town got its name was visible. Even the river, with varying duckweed, bladderwort, and water lily assortments, was greenish. Stephen often wished he had moved there with his brother, but then remembered his childhood friends in his hometown. A tear came to his cheek, thinking of all those people. There was no chance he would ever see any of them again; it left a large void in his chest. Thinking on the subject made him more lustful for revenge.

It took them a while of walking down several side streets, but they eventually came across a building that stood out; it held a slightly different shade of green than the others. A sign over the door read "John's Shoppe."

"This is it," said Stephen with a flourish of his hand, motioning towards the door. "My brother owns the place." They entered quietly, slightly nervous about entering a store in a different city. True, it was supposedly owned by his brother, but how was Stephen to know what kind of company his brother kept?

The main room was tiny, comprised of a small standing and browsing area for the customers, a thick oaken countertop, a place for the shopkeeper to stand, and a few shelves that held assorted wares on display; indeed, in all appearances, it was just an ordinary shop. A door in the center of the back wall led to a back room where the inventory was likely stored. Behind the counter stood a man remarkably similar to Stephen, though the two could only see the back of his head; he was facing the back wall, putting what seemed to be some new item arrivals on the shelves. Upon hearing the door open, he stopped what he was doing and turned around. "Hello, welcome to John's Shoppe. How may I help you?" Upon brief inspection of his new customers, one was recognized. "Steve?"

Stephen nodded and smiled warmly. "Yes, John, it's me!"

John hadn't seen or spoken with his brother in years, not due to any sort of disagreement; rather, it was blamed on the distance between their two towns. This was a big deal for the older shopkeeper. He raised his arms in greeting. "Steve! How've you been? Long time, no see!"

"I've been better," Stephen replied honestly, averting eye contact for a brief instant before returning it. "How are you?"

John noticed the strange action but didn't comment. "Great! Business isn't fantastic right now, but I get a few regulars who fancy themselves adventurers. What brings you here?"

Stephen shrugged. "Why else does one walk into a store? We need supplies."

This confused John slightly. "Well, thanks for the loving reunion scene. Why not get supplies at Springsboro?"

Stephen could have won an award for the way he restrained himself from breaking down, his face a perfect wall of stoicism. Angelo's facade had no difficulty cracking, however.

"Well, see, that's the reason we're here . . ." Stephen began. In spite of his magnificent performance, he was having a bit of difficulty stating their purpose; he knew, however, that his brother had to know of the terrible atrocity that had befallen his hometown. "John, there's nothing left of Springsboro. It was burned to the ground."

The brother raised an eyebrow. "Burned to the ground? What do you mean?"

"John, it's gone. Springsboro . . . it's gone. Something came, and when we got back . . ."

John was at a loss for words, a mixture of feelings and emotions welling up inside him. He experienced rage, sorrow, remorse, sadness, and desire for vengeance within a fraction of a second, and each moment of time brought with it new pain, new isolation. It felt to him like an eternity. All of his childhood memories, now gone up in smoke, quite literally. *It couldn't have been* him, thought John. *It had to have been someone else . . . This can't possibly be what he wants me to do . . .* At a loss for words, he soon realized he was also at a loss for breath. When he began to breathe again, the sudden oxygen flow to his brain was so strong that he fainted.

John's first words after he came to shocked Stephen greatly. "I'll give you all the supplies you need for free under one condition—I come on the journey."

"You? Why? Don't you need to keep an eye on things here?"

John sat up and began shouting, upset at the question. "Oh, come on, Steve! I grew up there, and now it's been destroyed! I have to do something, even if it turns out to be fruitless! I need this quest, and you need supplies. It's a win-win situation. I can help."

"Really?" This was the first time Angelo had spoken since entering the store; his arms were crossed in front of him defiantly, distrustful of this new figure. "What skills can you offer to aid our cause?"

John had not expected this obvious opposition, especially since he didn't recognize this new friend of Stephen's; it had been years since his parents had died and he decided to move here. Nonetheless, he listed what came to mind. "I can offer you supplies and the knowledge of how to use them. I'm also skilled at the crossbow, which can reach much longer distances than your longsword." He motioned at the sheath on Angelo's belt. "It could come in handy."

He has a point, thought Angelo. They could probably use a long-range weapon. As far as Stephen knew, they really had no money anyway. "Very well; in that case, I have no problem with you joining our cause," he lied. "Stephen?"

"Of course he can join! He has just as much of a right to be upset at this as either of us do."

"Thank you both so much!" John exclaimed. "As agreed, I'll give you the provisions we'll need for this journey. But let's leave that for tomorrow; it's getting late. Why don't the two of you stay at my place for the night?"

Stephen gaped at the offer. "Seriously? You sure we won't be too much of a burden?"

"I have a guest bedroom, and I can provide food. What am I supposed to do, let my brother sleep in the wilderness when I have perfectly good lodging?"

"Well, it *is* getting late, and we could use the rest," Stephen agreed. "Besides, who are we to refuse my brother's hospitality?"

*   *   *

The denizens of Feuerschloss found the scene playing before them to be highly amusing.

"Ha! Hospitality," sneered Asmodeious, "is for the meek. Diablo, stay here and watch the situation. I'm expecting a call on my mirror."

"Will do, sir."

Asmodeious hurried downstairs to the room directly below Diablo's lab. Nothing was allowed to be kept in this room save for a single mirror hanging in the middle of the wall opposite the door. The mirror had a gold tint to it, with pure ivory carvings making up the frame. At its zenith, the face of a dragon was carved, while down the sides were all the pernicious deeds done by Asmodeious by the time he was a hundred years old. The mirror was a gift to him, given many centuries ago by a Grecian sorcerer. The mountainfolk always did know how to combine ivory and gold in the most pleasing manner. As Asmodeious had expected, a message came through about five minutes upon his arrival.

"How'd it go?" he joked.

"I believe it went splendidly," John replied on the other end of the line. "He won't suspect an . . . enemy traveling with him."

Asmodeious chuckled lightly. "Good. Where is he now?"

John shrugged. "I don't know, probably asleep. Am I my brother's keeper?"

"Yes, for now. Now, where is he?"

"I just told you, he's gone to bed as far as I know." He changed the subject abruptly to one he wanted to discuss much more. "Look, when do I get my reward for doing this?"

Asmodeious snarled. "When he is no longer a threat. Remember, do not kill him yet. It may not be worth it. In the meantime, I'll be preparing a little something for those two. Asmodeious, out."

The mirror flickered off. Asmodeious allowed himself a hearty laugh, which quickly turned into a joyfully satanic bellow. *Now*, he thought, *it is time to put to use the things I got in the woods today.*

5

Elemental

After gazing at his collection of relics once again, Asmodeious returned to the pedestal on which his spellbook rested. Only one item remained—the jackolope horns. He had made enough of the substance to produce all five varieties of elemental summoners. After throwing in the final ingredients, he began the incantations.

He uttered a few nonsensical words that reminded him of the blaze he had started earlier that day; a translucent stone alive with fire flew out. Next, he expressed the feel of rigidity, solidity, and strength in sound he had never understood; a translucent stone the very definition of stone flew out. Asmodeious blinked, slightly confused at this development, then continued.

The sound of foamed crests crashing against wave breaks, of torrential downpours colliding with the firm yet gentle stream on its way to the ocean, screeched from his mouth; this stone seemed as though it would disappear and be at complete and absolute peace when thrown into a river. He emitted a sound that would make the very wind stand still, understanding and relating; the resulting rock felt as though it could be carried away on the clouds, though it had a definite weight.

The next and final words held the most difficulty for Asmodeious' admittedly limited larynx. Slowly so as to make sure he had them correct, he proclaimed the infinity of the Universe, praised the light of a myriad stars, and told the tale of galaxies long deceased; a stone black as night, a pitch so deep it could make the most steady star collapse, flew out. After the final jewel was in hand, a bracelet of purest gold flew from the remnant concoction. The five stones, in their order of creation, attached themselves to holes on the bracelet. Asmodeious slipped it over his wrist. A rush of power combined with adrenaline filled him brim-full with excitement. He wanted to try it right away.

A candle mounted on the wall burned innocently, lighting the farthest corners of the lab. Asmodeious, looking at it, decided it might be a good idea to start small. Staring at the flame and concentrating as hard as he could, he shouted "Fire!"

The candle flickered at the air coming out of his mouth but did nothing else.

Unsure of what he had done incorrectly, he quickly consulted the book. Realizing from where the problem stemmed, he slammed his forehead with his palm, expressing his frustration at his own inability to reason. This time, he thrust out the arm with the bracelet on it as he shouted the word once again. The red stone glowed and the flame on the candle grew, both in size and brightness. It flickered, and a flame leaped out.

The flame was a mere four inches tall. By the time it hit the floor, it had developed arms, legs, and a head. The first elemental had been created. Asmodeious went back and consulted his book to see what use he could make of this diminutive puppet. It gave an illustration of an elemental that looked remarkably similar to the one currently on the lab floor; underneath the picture, a series of commands and the resulting actions were listed in a sort of chart. The first few were detailing basic motor functions—walk, jump, skip, throw, and duck, to name a few. Any bipedal creature could perform such movement. Asmodeious soon grew bored of reading all the commands for this common locomotion. As he continued to read, the lettering and spacing seemed to get smaller and smaller. He closed his eyes and shook his head; the writing returned to normal. He skipped to the next page, near the middle. There, he observed a set of orders that were type specific to the fire elemental. Many looked interesting, and he even chuckled at a few. He decided to try some out, testing the bounds of the newfound slave. Pointing at it, Asmodeious made his first command.

"Burn, baby, burn!"

The elemental's flame began burning bright white, shedding light all over the room. The temperature of the chamber rose considerably. Pleased with the result, Asmodeious looked for the next test command; he found several that, when combined with the order he had already made, would create compounded effects. He decided on one of these.

"Disco inferno!" The miniature blaze started shedding white flashing sparks. Watching the whole charade, one might believe that the lab had transformed into a dance hall. The temperature noticeably rose again. A thermometer on the wall made of specific heat-resistant material read around 855 K. The mage was truly enjoying every minute of it; however, he wanted to test the rest of the elemental summoners.

Asmodeious found a vial of water that he had filled during a visit to Sapphire Ocean. He poured a small fraction of the water into a bowl and, thrusting the bracelet-gilded arm toward the bowl, shouted "Water!" The blue jewel glowed, while the water in the bowl formed. Soon, a little wet effigy jumped out. It looked like a crude human, only made entirely of water. Again, Asmodeious referred to his spellbook for commands. He wanted to see what it could do to the flame. He chose to go with the most deadly command to the fire.

"Extinguish!" The drippy drone ran to the far wall of the laboratory, grabbed the fire extinguisher from its mount, pointed it quite expertly at the fire elemental, and sprayed. The flame was indeed doused. Asmodeious blinked, shrugged, and decided to try a few more commands from the book.

"Puddle!" The creation collapsed into a puddle.

"Geyser!" It erupted from the ground with the force of the phenomenon it was mimicking.

Again, a feeling of power rushed over Asmodeious, making him rather light-headed. He could imagine the influence he could have on the people of this land. He might even be able to take over the highest seat of authority, if he so desired. He felt giddy; it was almost like being drunk, he noticed.

He was considering demonstrating to the water elemental exactly what it felt like to be drunk when a ringing sound echoed from upstairs. Somewhat disappointed, Asmodeious looked out the window, expecting to see dusk; instead, he witnessed dawn. His work had lasted throughout the night. Only when this truth finally sank in did he realize how tired he was. Had it not been for the incessant ringing of the mirror, he could have gone to sleep that instant. He trudged up the stairway, around the corner, down the hall, and into the mirror room, answering the call somewhat distractedly as he closed the door. "Hello."

"Hey, Asmodeious; it's me, John."

He was having difficulty holding his eyelids up by this point, but considering the source of the call, it might be something important. "What do you want?"

"Well, my brother wants to gather supplies and hit the road early this morning."

Asmodeious paused, waiting for more of an explanation. When it was obvious it wasn't coming, he scratched his head in frustration. "So?"

John was flustered; hadn't Asmodeious made the obvious connection yet? "So, I won't be able to communicate with you if we leave!"

Asmodeious had forgotten in his sleep-deprived state that John still didn't quite know how to work the mirror; he had only obtained it the day before, so it was only natural for him to not know what to do with it. "Alright, here's what you do. Break a piece of the mirror off. We can talk to each other through the shard. When you get back, just put the piece back where it was broken off, and the mirror should heal itself."

John was obviously completely confused as to how the hell the mirror worked, but his curiosity took a back seat to relief for the time being. "Thanks for the tip; I'll do that!"

"Whatever. Was that all?"

"Yes, my lord."

"Asmodeious out."

*   *   *

"John! Come on! Where are you? We should leave as soon as possible!" Stephen was searching the unfamiliar building high and low for his brother to no avail; he didn't seem to be anywhere. "John! Seriously, we need to get going!"

"I'm over here!" John emerged from around the corner.

"Where have you been? I've searched the whole house for you! Granted, it is rather large, but I didn't know where to look first!"

"Sorry; I had to take care of something. Shouldn't we be getting under way?"

Stephen almost objected to point out he had already said that, but realized quickly that the trip would commence more swiftly without such petty arguments and kept his silence. As the trio walked down the street back towards John's shop, Angelo hung behind.

I'm still not sure we can trust this guy, he pondered. First, he's human. *Sure, Steve is, too, but I've learned to trust Steve after several years; he's truly a good guy.* Humans in general, however, could not so easily be trusted; they always sold out too easily. *Second,* Angelo reasoned, *he had been the first one to go to bed, and the one to wake us up in the morning.* What was that human saying? Early to bed, early to rise, something else rather. It couldn't be good. *Last, both the night before and this morning, I could have sworn I heard John talking to himself as though he were carrying on a conversation.* Conclusion: the man had to be insane. Angelo decided he would cautiously observe from a distance before getting too close.

When they got to John's shop, Stephen was taken to the inventory room in the back to choose a weapon. John's stock held a surprising variety, for a small town. A broadsword, with a simple buffed iron hilt and a scabbard of black cowhide and silver highlights, hung from a lower post. A wooden quarterstaff, with white silk braided along the middle to provide some grip, leaned against the wall in the corner. He almost chose a battle-axe, sporting a bronze blade inscribed with many decorative lines and icons, but then attempted to lift it. Not being able to do so, he nearly lost hope in choosing a weapon. Then, another item caught his eye.

A relatively small sheath lay on a wooden shelf. It appeared to be made of wood wrapped in brown sheepskin, with three separate compartments for blades. The hilt of the main blade was made of a deep mahogany, the butt comprised of silver in the shape of a dragon's head. As Stephen took it out, he noted its one-edged curved steel blade. The cutting edge held a concave curve towards the hilt and bent back around into a convex tip, while the other side only had one slight bend in it, towards the blade itself. There was a small nick in the bladed edge near the hilt. Stephen had no idea what kind of weapon it was, but he liked it.

"That," explained John, "is called a kukri. That particular one was named Amoras by its maker. The other two much smaller bits, one is a general-purpose knife and the other is meant for maintaining both blades. Every kukri traditionally comes with them."

"Cool," said Stephen, as he started to put it back in its sheath. He tried the name out, rolling it off his tongue. "Amoras."

"NO!" shouted John as he realized what Stephen was doing.

"What?" asked Stephen, confused. "What did I do wrong?"

John waved his arms frantically. "Don't you know the mythology behind the blade?"

"Well, seeing as this is the first time I've ever encountered one, I'd say probably not."

John hung his head in disbelief. His brother was the history buff, yet *he* was the one explaining the history of the knife. "Legend has it that if you take a kukri out of its sheath, it must go back in with blood on the blade. Otherwise, the blade is cursed and becomes useless, or something like that. That's what that little nick is for—when you take it out, you ensure that blood is on the blade by cutting your thumb on the nick."

"I guess that makes sense," said Stephen. He winced as he pricked his thumb, then replaced the blade. "Amoras *is* the correct pronunciation, right?"

"Yes. Now let's get the other supplies we'll need."

The group gathered up several days worth of food and supplies, including a single canvas tent, and set off on their way.

Emerald Forest isn't nearly as foreboding and ominous as it had been yesterday, noticed Stephen. *What about yesterday made it so unusual? Was it just the night approaching? No, that's not likely the cause . . .* Stephen knew it had been the feeling of someone watching him, but Angelo hadn't felt it. *Am I just going crazy? Surely there's more to it than that.*

6

The Revered

Seven obelisks stood above all other construction. No one lived in or around these structures, but they were worshiped nonetheless; when it was questioned why, the answer was always simply because they were the pinnacle. One day, when the people weren't there paying homage but were instead readying for winter, one of the obelisks was toppled. No one saw or heard it happen—they were all too busy to notice anything like that at the time. Another, not a half an hour later, did the same thing. When the people finally noticed this calamity, they were devastated; a watch was set up to ensure nothing like this would ever go unseen again. Sure enough, the next night, one of the obelisks moved as though it was toppling. Most of the people assigned the task of watch rushed forward and attempted to brace the structure with their bodies, hoping they would be the ones recognized as the heroes. One man, however, took note of how the obelisk was falling: it appeared to be collapsing in the direction of a fourth tower. He then noticed that the other structures had fallen away from this one, as though something had forced them down. His hypothesis was insane, he knew; no one would ever believe him. He preached it anyway. As predicted, the people didn't listen; he was lynched, and his body was laid to rest on the mound of people who had died that night trying to support the obelisk. His was the body that finally cemented the obelisk; it could no longer move towards toppling its comrades, ensuring its own superiority above all others. Ironically, though it considered itself a failure, it was still the most worshiped of all. So goes the cycle, as much as it does it. As much as it does it. Asmus asit doesit. Asmosdesit. Asmodeious.

"Asmodeious, Asmodeious! Wake up!" Diablo shook his sleeping master violently.

"So goes the . . . cycle . . ." With a mighty yawn, the heavy sleeper rolled over, turning his back to the distraction. Diablo's attempts were not to be hindered, however.

"Asmodeious! I need you to wake up!"

"Huh, wha . . . What's wrong, Diablo?"

"Come here! I have to show you!"

Asmodeious followed the insistent apprentice, from his bedroom on the seventh basement floor to his open-air lab, the top of the structure. The only shelter this upper floor offered was a roof; this was where Asmodeious liked to practice some of his more menacing-looking magic, that the rest of the world might tremble if they happened to look in their general direction. At the moment, he would have liked to use it as a bedroom. Rightfully upset, he turned to the half-orc. "Now, what exactly is it you wanted to show me?"

Diablo pointed. "Over there, in the East."

Asmodeious' weary eyes followed a perfect line from Diablo's extended finger towards the East—a stunning feat for one so deprived of sleep. "I see the mountains, a desert, two huge trees, and a storm, all the usual things I see when I look out that way. What's so strange about that?"

"Sir, that storm is *coming* from that direction! That's the opposite direction of the ocean; the wind is blowing it the wrong way!"

"My, that *is* strange," yawned Asmodeious, his words dripping with sarcasm. He rolled his eyes, annoyed. "Wake me when there's a real emergency."

"But Asmodeious—"

"No 'but's! I'm going back to bed." He trudged down the stairs back into the castle. Diablo could only stand in the doorway, watching the storm approach. He understood meteorology, even if it was only a meager understanding. He knew from the desert below that storms traditionally came from the ocean to the West and got drained of their moisture by the mountains before it could reach the lands below; people who studied this sort of thing called it something akin to "rain shadow," he recalled reading. There was most definitely something wrong here, and if the master wasn't going to find out what, then the apprentice most certainly would.

The storm was extraordinarily large and dark, with an occasional lightning bolt illuminating the center. The darkness and flashes, mixed with the gallons upon gallons of water being dumped upon the Forest of the Unknown, then the Grassy Plains, and finally the Desert and the mountains, looked to Diablo like mobs of people sacrificing themselves, flying downward to their deaths for a purpose he did not understand. A fascinatingly swift storm for the knowledgeable mage, it arrived above the castle within the quarter hour. When the center passed directly above, Diablo disappeared.

*   *   *

It was about ten in the morning, and the Doe-Villalobos troupe had just arrived at the main road. The late morning sun shone through the translucent leaves in the trees, providing them the crystalline nature the forest was named for. Everyone was feeling confident except Angelo, and he couldn't see how the other two could continue with such certainty. They had no idea where to go; they didn't even know what it was they were looking for. "So, guys, hate to burst your bubble and all, but where exactly are we going?"

John, the only one of the three who actually knew where the roads in the forest led, was the one to answer. "Topaz City. There's an airport there wherein we can catch a flight to Flood City."

"Flood City?" Stephen recognized the name. "Isn't that the biggest city in the world?"

John nodded. "And the oldest."

Stephen became obviously excited. "All right! This'll be great!" He had always been the fan of history in every group he'd been in; the fact that their trek would take them to a city he had always wanted to go to made his month. "When does the plane take off?"

"We shouldn't be getting there until about eight this evening, so we need to find accommodations until morning. The plane will probably take off in about twenty-four hours, if I recall the flight schedules from my shipping lines."

Stephen could hardly contain his joy. He had always held an interest in ancient cultures, but the culture that once lived in the area of Flood City, known as the Assimmians, especially caught his eye. As a child, he had read everything he could find about them and aspired to become an Assimmiologist when he grew up. He never lost his fervor for studying the marvelous, mysterious civilization. He continued down the road with a newfound bounce in his step.

Angelo, on the other hand, was still wary. John had answered the question for sure, but he had successfully dodged the true issue at hand.

Why were they going to Flood City? How would doing so aid their quest? It had been a long while since he had seen a map, but he was pretty sure Flood City was to the southwest, almost directly perpendicular in direction to where they were wanting to go. This made no sense. Still, he decided it was better to tag along for now. Maybe John really did know more than he let on; perhaps there was a very good reason for visiting such an old, seemingly-irrelevant land. Besides, the airplane trip would certainly help if it were close enough to the necessary route anyway.

*   *   *

When Diablo finally came to, he looked at his surroundings with awe. Somehow, he didn't think he was anywhere near Feuerschloss any more. White, Romanesque columns held aloft a domed ceiling of what appeared to be fine-polished red Deltanian marble. Light filtered through a single hole at the zenith, diffusing a very calm, peaceful feeling. The mage had never experienced anything like it before in his life. He didn't especially like it.

Behind him, it was made obvious this was a floating structure; the floor suddenly and sharply dropped off around the otherwise relatively-small room. Before him, a hall stretched ahead. He decided, with little other choice, to explore this passage. On either side, the column motif continued; bright white clouds floated almost stoically outside. He had seen pictures similar to this depicting what the artists had referred to as "heaven." He wasn't particularly fond of those images, and this was no exception. Still, he was here with no way of knowing how to leave other than jumping to an untimely death, so he trudged onward.

An opening at the end of the hallway exited into one of the biggest rooms Diablo had ever seen. The floor was circular in shape, inlaid with what appeared to be an intricately detailed star map and Zodiacal calendar painstakingly crafted of varying semi-precious gems. Around the room supporting the gargantuan ceiling were further columns; these, however, were much taller and more stout than the previous ones. The ceiling itself was an impressive hanging gardens comprised of seven tiers, each one seeming to be supported by the plants beneath. The vivid colors of the blossoms were reminiscent of stained-glass windows, and the light reflected off the floor gave them an opalescent sheen.

To the left and the right were two more hallways, appearing to be structurally the same as the one Diablo had come through. Before him stood six thrones, made of unusual materials. He could hardly believe some of them, but they clearly existed nonetheless. On the farthest left, a throne of purest water was formed. Next to that was a chair so brilliant Diablo had to avert his eyes for a moment. The following throne seemed to have just grown up out of the ground as a calculated system of vines. The seat right of center was the most normal of the six, carved of fine granite from what looked to Diablo like the Eastern foothills of the mountains in which he and Asmodeious resided. Second from the end, the next throne was almost invisible were it not for a slight haze outlining it; Diablo wagered it was some kind of force field. The final throne seemed to have been manufactured haphazardly of layers of sod.

Seated on the thrones were individuals of lofty yet humble dispositions, their visages the very definition of noble. The one seated on the throne of sod spoke first. A gnome adorned in a finely-woven brown tunic, his sincere smile seemed almost a sneer as he stared directly at the confused half-orc in . . . was that admiration?

"Diablo Villalobos."

Diablo dared not speak, lest he be smitten by these obvious magic-users. This was a habit brought on by the wrath of Asmodeious, and a habit that had kept him alive. The six clearly expected him not to speak anyway, as the one seated on the throne of water began reciting next. Diablo recognized her species from tattered images that adorned some of the underused chambers of Feuerschloss; she was an elf, the first he had ever seen in person. Her clothing was minimal, yet she carried an almost motherly nature.

"Impressive, isn't it?" she said as she motioned towards the decorations Diablo had been examining only seconds before. "However, you weren't brought here for architectural sampling, as I'm sure you realize. Do you know the reasoning behind this action?"

Diablo responded to the question as honestly as he could. "No, I don't."

The bald halfling on the throne of vines, his eyebrow raised in a thoughtful manner, was the next to question him. "Do you know who we are?"

He shrugged. "To tell you the truth, I haven't the slightest."

The six suddenly began whispering fervently amongst themselves, apparently surprised by this response. As the minutes crawled by, Diablo's patience dwindled—he wanted answers from them, not questions. Why exactly *had* he been brought here? "Can you please tell me what this is all about?"

A rather menacing-looking half-orc answered from the throne of granite. "We're sorry, but your ignorance of our identity threw us off. Your life of solitude has probably left you oblivious to the rest of the world."

Life of solitude? Did they not know of Asmodeious?

"The elders of many societies ken us as the Revered," he continued. "We govern the many forces of nature with magic passed down to us by our predecessors. Our titles are . . ." He motioned toward the elf on the throne of water.

"Miranda," she said in a dulcimer soprano, "of water."

"Luna," continued the half-elf beside her, "of the moon and sky."

"Dryad," replied the halfling on the vines, "of the forest."

"Rhox," said the half-orc on the throne of granite, "of the earth."

"Chevron," answered the dwarf on the throne of air, "of the wind and air."

"And I," said the gnome seated on sod, "am Manas of the plains."

"We have brought you here," started Luna with a flourish of her bejeweled hand, "because one force still escapes our abilities. You, however, have mastered the art of magic and have the same unusual affinity for this force that each of us shares for our own."

"So, what are you saying?" asked Diablo, still uncertain of what was going on. "Why am I here?"

Chevron answered this question. "Diablo, we the Revered would like to extend unto you an invitation. Please, join our ranks as one of us, and we shall be eternally grateful."

Diablo was shocked by the proposition. What had he done that was worthy of joining this organization? He pondered his circumstances for a good long while, making sure to fully understand what was unfolding before him. *Would this benefit me? What if they find out about Asmodeious? I wonder where those young men are on their trail of revenge.* Finally, he came up with a legitimate question to ask the six. "What exactly is this force?"

"This force," answered Manas, "is fire."

"In that case, I accept your invitation."

"And we," replied Miranda, "accept your assent."

Each member of the Revered lifted his or her right hand, each of which began glowing with an almost internal light. "This one, who has accepted our offer, we accept into our circle, and thus, the circle of nature. He is one of us now, and one with us." A beam of light came forth from each of their palms and rested upon Diablo. "We now christen him as Salamandro of fire, bestow upon him the honorable and righteous title of the Revered, and with it, all the rights and benefits held therein."

The glow died down, and silence fell upon the assembly. Miranda was the first to speak. "Arise, Salamandro of fire."

Diablo stood up warily, somewhat queasy from what had just transpired. He could feel new power coursing through him, a feeling he hadn't experienced for a very long time. *Truly,* he thought, *this shall be advantageous.*

"Welcome among the ranks of the Revered, Salamandro," exclaimed Dryad. "Let us celebrate the induction of our newest member, and the first fire-Revered in a long time!"

The celebration was short, as there wasn't much in the way of food or drink in the floating palace at the time (Rhox profusely apologized for this oversight, as it was apparently his turn to obtain supplies), but there was certainly merriment. Besides, it was getting dark on the ground outside by the time everything was finished and everyone desired to get back to wherever it was they had come from. Diablo bade them all farewell, then, having been told what to do before he left, jumped from the palace in the sky. Using a new spell he had learned through the induction, he transmuted himself into a shooting star and flew back toward Feuerschloss.

7

The Poor Wet Starving Mongrel

The group had finally reached Topaz City. Because the skies were growing dark as John had predicted, they immediately began searching around for an inn with a vacant room. Stephen protested quite loudly at not being able to explore the mines responsible for the city's historic growth boom and economic prowess, but John insisted there was nothing much to see anymore.

"Most of the shafts have been closed down and sealed anyway for being unsafe; there would be no point, especially not this late. Besides, if we don't start looking for a room now, we're going to miss out and be stuck on the streets for the night."

"If you insist." Stephen moped as they continued wandering the still-darkening city in search of some sort of boarding establishment.

It didn't take terribly long—with Springsboro's decimation, a large chunk of the crowd usually traveling through the city was taken out as well. Within the hour they had come across a fairly cheap-looking pub, called "The Poor Wet Starving Mongrel" by the sign hanging precariously above the door. The exterior walls were wooden, in an overlap pattern that would have looked very classy and popular in a lesser state of rot. A coat of paint might have made for a touch of elegance were it not utterly absent from the facade. The windows were not glass, as the trio had been accustomed to, but what was later identified as mica; Stephen had read about such windows having been used over a century ago, and usually only in dwellings too poor to afford the then staggering price of glass. To make matters even more awkward, the building was a flat, and the only one on the entire road. This suggested that most folks who owned the land along the lane had enough sense to tear down the buildings and rebuild when they had become dilapidated beyond repair. They stood nervously outside the building for some time, each debating internally whether to enter. John was the first to break the silence.

"So . . . do we go in?"

Angelo shrugged. "I've seen worse establishments in Springsboro; besides, we shouldn't squander the luck we had in finding this place; we may not be so lucky again."

While Stephen agreed with Angelo on the second count, he didn't seem to recall seeing worse in his life, much less in his hometown. He still threw in his lot with entering and inquiring about a room for the night. John, in complete ambivalence on the matter, made the vote unanimous.

A collective sigh of relief escaped as the three entered to find the interior at least structurally sound, complete with a still relatively-solid brick skeleton. Of course, the pub itself rewarded those who chose to judge based on external appearances. The dining area, if it could ever be called that, was filled with shoddy tables made of halved barrels and crudely-constructed tops. Each had at least one crooked nail sticking out somewhere, often more, and it was clear the tables were well-loved in spite of such construction. The bar, against the left wall from the entrance, also appeared to be what one might consider the reception desk for the boarding; it seemed the most properly-maintained part of the entire structure, almost perfectly level and showing few signs of deterioration in spite of what were surely ages of use. Behind it stood a large, older man who had obviously seen his share of brawls; a man of hardened features and many scars, he seemed more interested in being able to see through the bottom of the stein he was cleaning than attending to his newest first-time customers. Behind him in turn were several barrels, non-halved, full of what one could only assume was some form of spirits. Usually, as John already knew, in establishments like this, the type of liquor never mattered, as it was typically unfit for consumption anyway.

Taking the full sight in, the trio finally decided on an empty barrel-table away from most of the commotion and sat upon the rickety stools set around it, waiting for someone who knew anything about what they were doing to see to them.

"Y'all ain't from 'round here, are ya?" A man with an eyepatch, slimmer and, in spite of his obvious younger age, more bald than the bartender, approached their table.

"What gives you that idea?" inquired Stephen.

"Well, not really, no; you could say we're traveling for business," replied John quickly, attempting to quiet his less-traveled brother lest he accidentally incur the wrath of the man. "Am I to assume you're the waiter?"

"Ah, we got us a comedian here, ain't we? Ya, I'm the bloody waiter." The young man eyed John cockily, grinning thinly. "Our cook don't make but one thing a night, so y'all'll just have to enjoy it. Any of ya's wants a drink ta drown it with?"

John gave a look of disgusted apprehension. Stephen had partaken of alcohol on occasion, but nothing from a place as this. Angelo had never tasted the stuff.

"I suppose I'll take one, considering the circumstances; Stephen? Angelo?"

"I guess I'll try a bit," replied Stephen somewhat sheepishly.

The waiter laughed. "A bit? What are ya, a kid? Whatever, Just so's ya ain't caught off-guard, all we gots are pints, so you're gonna have ta suck it up and take it like a man. What about the overly-talkative half-elf 'ere; what'll it be?"

"I consider alcohol a poison. Please serve me accordingly."

The waiter gripped at his patched eye lightly, bringing his head down into a full guffaw. "Y'all're some odd folks, I'll grant ya. I think I like that. Fine, that'll be three chef's specials and two pints, coming right up."

"Err—" began John, hoping to stop the waiter before he disappeared.

"What, did I get it wrong? Or do ya desire a double-helpin'?"

"Actually sir—"

"Name's Mike, man."

"—Mike then, we were also hoping for . . . lodging? For the night?"

"Oh, you gotta talk to that mass o' man behind the counter there. Name's Charlie; he'll get ya bedded what quick-like. I think we gots a room left. But yea, he's the guy ta talk to 'bout that." With that, Mike made for the kitchen.

The waiter returned swiftly with two pints full of a thick, dark-brown barely-liquid. Neither Doe was brave enough to try it at first, but curiosity finally got the best of Stephen.

"How does it taste?" inquired John.

Stephen took a minute. "Well, having never tasted the contents of a spittoon, I can't truly say for certain, but I can say that *if* I were to do so—"

"Thank you, that's enough."

After a relatively quiet twenty minutes of waiting around, the waiter returned again with three plates of a barely-identifiable substance. To eat this stuff could be considered a bit of a miracle. Stephen thought it looked like old, stringy beef with sautéed onions, while Angelo thought it looked more like rotting lamb topped with mushrooms. John tried not to think about what it was he was eating. This proved difficult after Stephen demonstrated that, with proper application, one could in fact remove paint with it.

Upon completion of the so-called meal, the three approached "Charlie" as instructed. The brute spoke with a scratchy baritone, the tone implying quite strongly that he may have been the primary source of most of the smoke in the building. "Wha' kin Ah do fer ya gents?"

"Charlie, I presume?" began John. "Mike told us you were the man to talk to about lodging."

"Lodgin'? Do ya per'aps mean a ROOM?" Charlie pulled a ponderous tome out from under the counter and dropped it heftily upon the surface, a cloud of dust bursting from the underused text. "Ya, we kin accommodate. How many ya want?"

"Oh, err, just one would do us for the night sir."

"No 'sir' 'ere, man; Charlie's fine. One room? Ya gots . . . room one, then. Hallway, left. Kin't miss e'." Nodding in appreciation to the surprisingly genial barkeep, the three went to their room. Once there (Charlie had been correct; it had been in fact the only room on the left), they deposited their belongings and got ready for bed, which included for some the act of throwing up. They subsequently tried to get some sleep after such a long day of travel. As he was falling asleep, Angelo could have sworn he heard John talking to himself again. Now it was keeping him up. Stephen, however, fell asleep right away, and within minutes, was dreaming.

A mountain range was in the distance. Smoke seemed to be bellowing from the peak of one. Suddenly, a meteor struck the side of the mountain. A massive amount of magma poured out and was flowing towards him. To his left was Angelo, ready to attack. To his right was John, wearing a two-toned jacket with the colors split down the middle. He himself was standing like a mannequin, unable to move. Behind him was someone he had never met in his life, but was determined to help. The lava kept coming and coming, until . . .

Stephen woke up in a cold sweat. Who was that man? Why couldn't he move? Why did the lava flow towards them? Why was John wearing that ridiculously gaudy jacket? He had so many questions, and he felt that he would find the answers soon enough.

8

Flight

It was early morning. Asmodeious had woken up much earlier, when an impact from what looked like a meteorite shook the ground enough to bring the magma level up to his bedroom. It did not rise enough to cover his head, but it was enough for him to start feeling mildly uncomfortable.

His little nap had lasted for about eighteen hours; he was not fully rested, but he was rested enough to start thinking of ways to hinder the progress of the group of three. He had memorized their names, and it was the one called Stephen who truly worried him. At the rate they were going, they had probably reached Topaz City by now, he thought to himself. With John as their guide, though . . . He decided to pay Diablo a visit in his lab. His cauldron would come in handy after all.

After climbing the eight flights of stairs to reach the second floor, Asmodeious walked down the hall and knocked on the door to Diablo's lab. There was no answer. He banged again, harder. Still, there was no answer. "Diablo! Are you in there!?" he shouted as he beat the door a third time. Once again, no one answered. He decided to look in.

The room was as it had been when Asmodeious had last left it, now almost two days ago. Something was amiss. Diablo always loved making little trinkets, and nothing new was on the shelf. Oh, well. Asmodeious had come for the cauldron. Diablo would tell him if something was wrong later.

Asmodeious touched the surface of the silvery liquid. He stated the password, which then led him to looking at himself. He changed the radius until Topaz City came into view. Then, he zoomed in on a single pub room, where three intrepid adventurers were preparing for a lengthy flight.

*　　*　　*

"Sixty-seven Moktles!" John screamed in disbelief. "We were told that the room would only cost us thirty-two!"

"Well," began Charlie, "th' room did only cost ya thirty-two. Ya requested a cot, which costs ya five, the meal were free wit' a stay, and th' repair costs thirty."

"Repair? What did we break? What *could* we have broken, in this place?"

"There were damage done to one o' th' walls o' th' pub, Jack. We have ta pay for new paint, an' the cleaning supplies ta get th' rest o' th' mess off the wall. Th' paint'll cost fifteen, an' th' supplies an' labor'll make up th' rest o' th' cost o' th' sixty-seven."

John muttered something rather hateful and rude under his breath as he dug out his wallet and forked over a third of the money. The man behind the counter cleared his throat. "This ain't nearly enough."

"I know," John said to the increasingly-annoyed barkeep. "Guys, do you mind helping me out here? I need another forty! You stayed here, too, and should at least help with the costs! Stephen, you were the one who did the most damage, you should pay the most!"

They both whined, reached into their pockets, and gave Charlie the rest of the money. "Thank ya gents," he said as he put it into the cash register. "Ya have a nice day."

"Man," Stephen whispered to Angelo. "With prices like this, we deserve the towels I swiped!"

John made no comment, but headed straight for the door as swiftly as possible.

Once the trio was outside and down the road a little ways, John started to speak again. "Guys, I'm completely tapped. That place took the last of my money. Do either of you have anything left?"

"I'm broke, too," said Stephen.

"Actually, I've still got fifty Moktles left."

John stared in disbelief, for the second time that day. "You've been holding out on us? Well, I suppose it's for the better. We'll need every decan of that to get us to Flood City on the plane."

"Where is the airport, anyway?" Stephen asked.

"Well, look on the map. Surely it's labeled."

"Umm . . . what map?"

John paused. "I had given you a map at my store. I said to hold on to it, lest it get lost."

"I thought Angelo had it as we left the pub."

"Well, crap." John was not in a good mood to begin with, and now this was making it worse. "You left the damn map in the room, didn't you?"

"I guess . . ."

"Well, it's gone! We set foot in that place again, and they'll charge us another night, which we most definitely cannot afford."

Stephen thought about this for a short while, then said, "Why don't we ask one of the residents? Surely they know where the airport is, seeing as they live in this city."

"Whatever you think would be best," shrugged John.

So Stephen looked around for any random stranger on the street. An older-looking man, perhaps in his mid-forties, happened to be approaching them on their side of the road.

"Excuse me, sir," started Stephen, "but could you direct us towards the airport? We're from out of town, and don't really know our way around."

"Why certainly," said the older man. "Just go straight down this street, then take a right at the third intersection. It should just be at the end of that street, if I remember correctly. If not, then that's at least close to it, and you should be able to find it by the noise."

"Thank you very much! Let's go, John!"

They followed the man's instructions, and it led them straight to the airport's front gate. All they had to do now was purchase passage for the three of them and find their plane. As it was still only nine in the morning, they had a little bit of time. They weren't too worried about that. Angelo paid for the tickets, which totaled quite miraculously to fifty Moktles exactly. They were now officially out of money. The only thing they could afford was a small, private sort of plane leaving at ten. This just happened to be the flight John was hoping for.

Stephen was the first on the plane. He seemed a bit overly excited about finally getting to fly. It was something he'd wanted to do all his life, but was only just getting the chance. He was ecstatic; more so than usual, which somewhat frightened Angelo. Through all the excitement, no one had realized the pilot had just gotten in.

"Hello, everyone!" The sudden welcome took Angelo by surprise. "My name is Dave. I'll be your pilot on this flight to Flood City. I hope you enjoy yourselves!" With that, the flight safety video started playing on a small monitor in the front of the room.

*   *   *

The invention of the airplane came about by the actions and intentions of a smith from Topaz City. A dwarf, the young Latham Brander despised the ancestral ties his kind held with the earth and longed since childhood to remove himself from the racial rut he had been placed in by birth. At the age of six, he began noticing the various subtle nuances of air currents, recording each differing caress of the wind in what would later become his greatest written contribution to the world—an exhaustive tome on atmospheric flow and the manipulation thereof. When he entered his apprenticeship, the bellows would provide his first inspiration to attempt magic, focusing on creating a pressure gradient so his forge would never go cold while he was working.

It was when he first traveled to Monsoon City on a errand from his master that he observed how differing locations had naturally-varying overall air current systems; specifically, he was shocked to find that this southern city had an incredibly strong stream from the southwest that split almost perfectly against the cliffs that rose above the borough to the east, forming their face so absolutely evenly as to make them near impossible to scale. It was from this that he began mapping out the world's naturally-occurring grand-scale air currents, looking for what might be the best location from which to leap into the wind and soar through his own brand of subtle pressure manipulation.

His answer, after almost five years of constant travel as a journeyman, was upon those very same cliffs. At the top point, the air provided a marvelous cushion upon which a metal craft might be easiest lifted. In a shack at the base of a mighty tree that grew removed enough from the edge of the cliff so as to not be distracted, but close enough to provide proper study of the various eddies of the wind, Latham devised and built his contraption, including in its very framework the necessary magic to provide the most surefire lift possible. On that day, it is said that every neck in Monsoon City was strained skyward at the emergence of the vehicle from the point. It flew for over a minute, coming to rest in a perfect landing in the middle of the public square. This first plane was donated to the people of Topaz City, for providing him with the work that inspired him so.

Two days after this first flight, Latham was approached by a group of wandering mages. Changing his name to Chevron in honor of the cliffs that helped him so, he joined their ranks and continues to be revered to this day.

*   *   *

Diablo woke up. His little journey had tired him to the point of exhaustion, and the turning-into-a-meteor bit didn't help things; when he landed, if that's what it could be called, he just collapsed into sleep for a few hours. He was rested well enough by this point to go check on things in his laboratory. He hadn't been there in a while, so nothing should be wrong with it; still he wanted to check the Cauldron to see if anything new had developed.

When he opened the front door, he was surprised to notice that there were no signs of Asmodeious. *Perhaps he was still sleeping*, Diablo thought. He quickly proceeded up to his lab, lest he encounter his master in the meantime. Opening the door, he noticed everything had been left as it was. He liked that—knowing that his privacy was secure, even when he was gone. Well, he had come to check the cauldron, so he went through the process of turning it on. He then flipped through the different dots on the map in the region of concern until he came across the faces he recognized. They were in an airplane.

The first leg of their voyage was complete already!? Diablo couldn't believe his eyes. They should not have been in that airplane yet. Surely there was something wrong with this situation; surely Asmodeious was out trying to stop this horrendous act. As he was thinking this, an anomaly caught his eye—another blip on the map in what appeared to be the restroom. He realized that John wasn't among those in the passenger seating area. He knew that John was Asmodeious' wild card, but how this was, he did not know. Perhaps this was where the plot thickened, he thought. He prodded this new dot.

Sure enough, John was not using the toilet. He appeared to be talking into his hand as though to another being. Turning the sound on, Diablo could make out a few tidbits of conversation that were truly useful.

"Yes, I know it's early . . . Don't worry about a thing . . . I have a plan once we get to Flood City . . . I know we weren't supposed to even get to the plane . . ."

After that point, Diablo stopped listening. He had all the information he needed to come up with a truly devious plan. If this worked, it could bring him up to par even with Asmodeious! One of the benefits of being a Revered he remembered from his induction was instant "telecommunication"—it wasn't quite telecommunication, as the user spoke the words, and the Revered who was meant to hear would be the only one to do so. It was a very useful trick that would come in handy at that moment. Diablo concentrated on contacting the one called Chevron.

"Chevron, do you hear me? This is Salamandro."

"Aye, Salamandro, I can hear you. Are you just testing all the new powers you've received? I mean, that's okay, everyone does—"

"No, I actually have sort of a dilemma that you could solve for me. You see, there's a plane traveling about due west of your tree right now, am I right?"

"Hold on, let me check . . . Yes, I see it."

"Well, that plane happens to carry passengers to Flood City who are bent on the destruction of the Revered."

"What!? How do you know this?"

"I have some very reliable sources. Even if their wrong, though, we cannot take that risk. Chevron, would you be able to blow them off course?"

"Of course. Anyone who collaborates against the Revered, whether in truth or tale, must be stopped!"

*　　*　　*

The plane began to shake violently.

"Don't worry folks," came the voice of Dave from the cockpit. "It's just a little turbulence. I'm going to ask you, for your own safety, to return to your seats, put them in their fully upright and locked positions, and to fasten your safety belts. We wouldn't want anyone getting hurt, now, would we?"

Stephen was worried about John. He'd been in the toilet for a good five minutes now. Was he okay? Was he going to be safe in there with all this turbulence?

And as Stephen began to truly worry for his safety, John returned from the bathroom as though to put Stephen's thoughts to rest.

"John, you have to—"

"I know, I heard. I'll sit down."

John sat down, and as he did, the plane rocked violently to the right. It knocked Angelo's head against the bulkhead, nearly knocking him unconscious. It was obvious from the way Dave was reacting that this was unusually strong wind. This should not have been happening. Then, as if things couldn't get any worse, the plane started to roll.

"Passengers, I have lost control of the plane. These winds are far too strong. We are going to crash. From our current trajectory, I would say that we are going to land in the Sapphire Ocean, so everyone needs to get their personal flotation devices from under their seat and start inflating them as in the safety video. Please remain calm."

Stephen's first thought was *crap, we're gonna crash, we're gonna die* . . . John, on the other hand, seemed slightly calmer. Angelo also seemed calmer, but he was mostly unconscious anyway. Dave did not bother hiding his fear. They were going down, with very little chance for survival.

9

Beachfront

Stephen was soaking.

That was all he could think of, was that he was wet. And his eyes were closed. The taste of salt suddenly made itself noticeable on his tongue. The ground felt unusually cold and murky, compared to his back, being toasted by an unseen heat. He finally thought to open his eyes. The ocean spread out behind him, shimmering in the much-too-bright sunlight. Before him was a large stretch of bleach-white sand, tinted only by the saltwater as it lapped the shore. This beach appeared to be well developed; there were several high-rise hotels lining the sand, and many small cabanas peppered the landscape. Countless umbrellas and towels scattered the beach, many with occupants. He then looked to his left and right, at the bodies not occupying any towels. Angelo and John had washed up as well. The pilot was nowhere in sight.

What had happened? He couldn't bring himself to remember immediately; it took quite a bit of backtracking. There was the plane, he remembered, and they were on their way to Flood City, trying to stop evil of some sort. Then, he remembered a large turbulence, then . . . Stephen shuddered despite the now pounding heat. He knew what had become of the pilot. Not wanting Angelo or John to befall the same fate, he dragged them up the slight incline out of the tide. As soon as they were safely away from the waves, he began giving resuscitation. Angelo woke next, coughing up quite a large sum of water.

"Wha . . . where are we?" he asked after he stopped gagging.

"To be honest, I have no idea," explained Stephen, "but we're alive and somewhere that probably offers medical aid of some manner." John wasn't waking up; it was worrying Stephen to the point of nervous breakdown. Surely there was enough air in him by this point to displace the water. He started to perform chest compressions. That was all required. John choked back to life.

"Whoa, man, you don't need to push so hard, I'm up!" Looking around, it was obvious that John also had no clue as to their whereabouts.

"Perhaps we could go to one of these cabanas and ask someone where exactly we are," suggested Angelo. "After all, they are here on purpose, supposedly."

"True," said John, "but they would probably assume the same of us and think us either crazy or having mischievous intentions."

"Yes," piped in Stephen, "but we won't know for sure unless we try. Besides, surely there are *some* nice people here." The trio eventually decided to give it a shot.

They chose a friendly-looking place called the "Copo Cabana" a few hundred feet up the beech. The doors were traditional swing-open doors that only half-covered the doorway itself, the kind one might expect in a nice, breezy, comfortable place on the seaside. As they walked in, Stephen took note of their surroundings, as did Angelo. John didn't seem to care too much.

The basic setup was such that in the back of the small dining room was an equally small bar, made of what looked like varnished yellowstone pine. The paint on the walls was almost the same color as the sky, and the wainscoting came up the walls about three feet. It, like the bar, appeared to be pine, as did the floor. The tables, round and scattered around the rest of the room, were made of a lighter wood, but were also varnished. The inhabitants of the tiny establishment were as varied as they came. One in particular caught Stephen's eye. He was just getting up from the bar.

From the back, the figure was hard to make out through the long dark blue robes. It appeared to be an elf of some years. The long hair, blonde, was noticeable from anywhere in the room; it appeared to have its own radiance. The figure wore no hat. As it turned around, Stephen made it out to be a male from the face, barely weathered with more experience than age, and a five o' clock shadow to match. One hand held a large wooden rod with a glass ball on the upper end; the other placed a small tip on the bar table. His eyes were a deep gray, though the edges hinted at a previous green. For a brief instant, he made eye contact with Stephen, but didn't appear to notice. Then, as he walked towards the door, he slowed and slightly glanced back. Where had Stephen seen that face before . . . It was now staring straight at him, studying him as he had done just moments ago.

"It's YOU."

Stephen shook his head in instant confusion. "What do you mean, it's me? I've never seen you before in my life, I don't think."

"No, you haven't," said the stranger; "we've not seen each other before this moment, but were destined to meet one day."

"Okay, pal," said John, putting his arms between the two in an attempt at separation. "I think you've had one too many drinks."

"You can check my blood alcohol level; I'm completely sober. You're Stephen Doe. You are the one who must help me. You are the only one who can."

"What do you mean? I've no idea what you're talking about."

The elf bowed, introducing himself to the trio. "My name is Justin. I am a wizard of the clan of Bailey, but only by blood relation. My magical abilities should be more than they are, but . . ." He looked around at the room of people now staring at them intently. "Let's discuss this more outside." They left the building and chose a place on the sand away from the large crowds.

"I was born into the clan of Bailey, the strongest house in magic, wizardry or sorcery. I'm not strong enough to keep my name from being permanently tarnished in their eyes. That's where you come in, Stephen. You need to help me learn to focus my magic so it can be stronger."

"Wait," started Stephen, "I'm supposed to help you with magic? I don't know the first thing about magic. I'm just a normal person."

Justin quirked an eyebrow. "This is a test, isn't it?"

"No, I'm quite serious."

"But it must be a test," protested Justin. "You are one of the most powerful magicians alive! I know of you by your dreams; they are so strong, they broadcast to those in them, if they know how to receive them."

"I've never known any of his dreams," objected Angelo.

"Well, I did say you had to be in them, and that you had to be open to reception."

Stephen was completely confused. He'd never known that he had abilities relating to magic in any manner. And just how had this Justin guy ended up in his dreams, anyway? Indeed, he realized where he had seen the elf's face—the dream he'd had just the night before. This was getting to be too freaky for words. Had they not already been sitting down, this is where Stephen would have done so.

As if he had read Stephen's thoughts, John spoke up. "Just how did Steve here know of you in order to have a dream with you in it? And why were you 'receptive'? Just what are you trying to pull here?"

"I understand your many questions. To be honest, I'm not sure I know why Stephen has had dreams with me in them. The reason I am receptive is that it *did* contain me, and any dream doing so is from the person destined to help me. I am only trying to improve my own abilities through the help of the one who is better."

"But I'm not better!" shouted Stephen. Then, noticing other people a few hundred feet down the beach staring at them, he quieted down. "Just how much magic do you know, anyway?"

"Well," Justin started, "this is kind of embarrassing. I can't perform any. I know a lot, but I just can't pull them off properly."

The other three collapsed in disbelief.

"You mean to tell us," questioned Angelo, "that you, being of no magical talent whatsoever but having the bloodline of countless great wizards, want help from an equally useless person when it comes to magic, simply because you claim to have seen his dream within your dream?"

"Yes! The half-elf gets it!"

"No, I don't!" Angelo sighed in a mixture of annoyance and frustration. "Look, the only reason we went into that little cabana was to find out where we were. Perhaps you would be so kind?"

"Yes, but thats something of an odd question. This is Cibola Beach, the largest beach in the known world. It's technically part of Flood City, but it's so large that many consider it to be a separate community altogether, and indeed it gets its own tax district."

"We're near Flood City!?" Stephen gaped in astonishment. "What a tremendous stroke of luck that we happened to wash up in the city that we needed to be in in the first place!"

Justin was slightly confused. "Washed up?"

"Uh, well, yeah, you see . . ." John tried to explain the situation. "We were originally in an airplane coming to this city from Topaz City, when we experienced some turbulence about halfway here, and our plane crashed in the ocean. The pilot died, or at least we can't find any trace of him."

"Halfway here from Topaz City, you say?" Justin had a look of deep thought.

"What's the matter?"

Justin took a second, then replied, "Do you remember seeing a rather large set of cliffs, or a massive tree near where you experienced the turbulence?"

"Now that you mention it," said Angelo, "I do remember thinking that such a large tree was kind of odd."

"Hmm . . ." Justin was clearly deep in thought at this development.

"Would you mind explaining exactly what the problem is?" asked Stephen in utter confusion. "What would a large tree have anything to do with the immense turbulence?"

"Here," Justin replied, beckoning the others to follow him. "I'll show you; the information is back at my place. Trust me, if my hunch is correct, this could be interesting."

The group of three wondered if this was such a good idea. "We don't have to go with him," thought John aloud to the other two. "In fact, if we only pretend to follow, we could even lose him."

"True," said Angelo, "but we need a room for the night, and we don't have any more money; we're lucky to have clothing and weapons at this point, as everything else went down with the plane. Perhaps he could help us there, too."

"Oh, you're just advocating him because he's an elf!" exclaimed John insinuatingly. "You elves always stick up for each other."

"Actually, John," said Angelo, massaging his temple, "I'm only half-elf. If anything, I wouldn't advocate him to save my life. We, however, do not have very many options. We could either go with him and take full advantage of this admittedly unusual situation, or we could go out on our own, get lost, and end up dead. Which would you prefer?"

I know what Asmodeious would prefer, John thought to himself. *I already got my ass handed to me once, and I'd rather avoid it again, but it would look suspicious if I were to say no to such an advantageous offer.* "Fine, let's go with him. Besides, all our provisions did go down with the plane; we could use some money and food, not to mention shelter."

Stephen didn't bother standing around for the argument. He wanted to find out more about this man who somehow knew of his existence, even with the obvious distance barrier and having never met before. And, if they had met before, sometime in the past, how had Stephen forgotten? He had so many questions, and knew that going with Justin to his homestead was the only way any of them were going to be answered.

*　　*　　*

Asmodeious came out of the mirror room with a satisfied grin on his face. He was originally upset at John for even letting the group get on the plane, but a freak bout of turbulence ended his worries once and for all, it seemed. That Stephen kid would never become a nuisance. He found a new bounce in his step as he went up to Diablo's lab to survey the damage. Today, he knew, was going to be a good day.

He had heard Diablo come in the door behind him some time ago. Perhaps he had been out with an important chore of some sort. Asmodeious didn't know, nor did he really care; Diablo would tell him everything new, which was part of the reason he was making the trek up the stairs even now. Beating information out of his apprentice was something he hadn't done in a while; it would be fun.

Rounding the corner at the top of the stairs, he pondered what Diablo could have been up to since they last crossed paths a day before. Surely it could not be so important as to try to sneak in without Asmodeious noticing. The sad thing about that idea was, Asmodeious noticed everything that went on within Feuerschloss. To try to get something around him was foolish; even a child would be able to see that, especially had they seen the real Asmodeious. It was a fearsome sight, to be sure, and Diablo had known it since infancy. He would never risk something like his life for a bit of information. It was unreasonable.

Asmodeious beat on the door in his usual manner. "Diablo!"

This time, the door opened slowly. Too slowly for Asmodeious' liking. He thrust open the door malignantly, looking around the room instinctively as he did so. He could never be too careful when Diablo was being cautious. Nothing appeared wrong, but he wanted to make sure. "Diablo, what's been going on?"

Diablo tried his best to feign ignorance. "Whatever could you mean?"

"Diablo, stop pretending; you're only embarrassing yourself. I know something's up; you came in rather early in the morning, unannounced, and proceeded here immediately. What is going on? I demand an answer! Where were you either this morning or last night!?"

Diablo had been frightened before by Asmodeious, but this time, he was ready to soil himself. Should he spill about the Revered? If he did, it would mean the end of their existence; Asmodeious hated any form of rivalry against himself enough to have it wiped out. If he kept it secret, however, it would only be a matter of time before Asmodeious found out the truth. Then, there would truly be Hell to pay. Diablo was torn between the two choices; he then remembered what he himself had just requested Chevron do. Quickly, he made up his mind.

"I went out this morning to investigate the large crash. Surely it woke you? Anyway, it was nothing more than, uh, a burst lava bomb, nothing big, so I just decided to take a nice walk, see what all was going on this morning in the underbrush. I came back quietly so as not to disturb you, knowing you were probably still asleep."

Asmodeious pondered this for a while. It was obviously a lie; Diablo hated walks in the forest. He wanted to keep something secret. While it upset him, Asmodeious was easily calmed by the idea that he could tell without a doubt that Diablo had lied. The revenge would only be all the sweeter. Asmodeious looked forward to it.

"Very well. The main reason I came up here was to see something in the cauldron. Something's . . . come up."

"Oh, you mean with that one group of three? I already saw. They crashed into the ocean. Pretty neat, if you ask me."

"Well, I desire to survey the damage myself." He walked over to the cauldron and set it to look at the now destroyed aircraft. Debris was everywhere; it had obviously hit at an incredible speed. Surely, no one could live through that, thought Asmodeious. *It's finished. I've won!* "HA! What luck, that such a strong freak wind like that would have taken out my greatest opposition!"

Diablo wanted to speak up, to let Asmodeious know who was responsible for the now twisted wreckage displayed before them, but knew he could not. It would reveal the very nature of his secret. No matter how it would make him look good, he couldn't risk it.

"Alright, now, to view their surely rotting corpses," announced Asmodeious. "View Jonathan Doe." The view switched to a busy-looking street in a rather large town. Asmodeious recognized the street layout as a much older part of Flood City, *but why would it show me this?*, he wondered. Then, the thought crossed his mind. *Impossible,* he thought. *No way anything could have . . .* He had to make sure. With a nervous gulp, he uttered the command, "Zoom in."

The camera began to zoom in towards a portion of the crowd that was rather small and unnoticeable. Everyone else seemed to go around this particular group. Soon, it was possible for Asmodeious, with his superb eyesight, to make out the individual faces on the four members of the traveling troupe. Sure enough, he could recognize Stephen, Angelo, and John, visibly roughed up but walking as though nothing had happened. They had escaped unscathed. Who was the man leading them? It didn't matter; nothing mattered anymore except the extermination of those three. Asmodeious let out a mighty bellow of anguish, anger, and frustration. *One way or another*, he thought, *I will win.*

10

Justin

"So," said Stephen, breaking the silence that resulted from arriving at Justin's home, "this is where you live? Well, I like what you've done with such an obviously tight budget."

It couldn't be called a house. Really, it couldn't be called a building; otherwise, it would fail enough safety regulations to be demolished, which wouldn't have been hard. Everyone had to make sure they didn't touch the walls so as to ensure they didn't create a similar fate. It wasn't as though they would have wanted to, anyway. The walls appeared to be made of oriented strand board crudely nailed together. The roof was one of those tin roofs, and it had holes in several places where no one had bothered to repair it. The place was obviously unsanitary; cockroaches and flies were so frequent that Justin didn't even flinch at their sight after a few seconds.

"Actually," retorted Justin, "I've got quite a large budget; however, the signs of a true wizard are humility and paying as little attention to the cleanliness of one's surroundings as possible. This usually means that the residing wizard spends all his time studying magic."

"Well, you could at least try to clean the place once in a while," said John, gagging disgustedly. "Like, say, once a month?"

Angelo didn't bother to open his mouth, partly because his opinion had already been expressed, and partly because he was afraid one of the flies would decide to fly in to a cleaner location.

Stephen, after slight exploration, was glad to find that there was a toilet connected to working plumbing fixtures, and that it had been used.

"To be honest, this is only my residence; I spend most of my time away, whether at the cabana or in Monsoon City. That's where my lab is. It's a city quite a ways north of us. If my thoughts are justified, you were almost directly over the city when you experienced the turbulence."

"Okay," said Angelo, trying to keep his mouth as closed as he could, "what do the tree and the cliffs have to do with our plane crashing? Now that we're here, you could possibly explain this to us, correct?"

"Ah, yes, I had completely forgotten that fact. Follow me." Justin beckoned them towards what looked like a stairway to a bomb shelter. *Let's just hope the bomb that went off up here didn't have any effect down there,* thought John. *We do need a place to sleep without dying.*

Luckily for them, the "basement" was much cleaner; clean enough to possibly make into a makeshift sleeping quarters. Angelo realized that that was exactly what this was with a glance to the corner of the concrete bunker; a cot, complete with pillow and blanket, were set up and disheveled enough to have been used recently. The house above was probably just for show, he realized. Had any other wizards come to visit, they'd think he was one of the most dedicated in the field.

In the center of the room was an oddly-shaped altar of some sort. It had seven sides to it, each with a different picture. From where Angelo stood on the stairs, he could see a picture depicting a raindrop, a tree, and what looked to be the sun. Each side also had a recessed portion to it, as to suggest the placement of something. As though to answer the question of what, he could make out a few traces of wax, probably having dripped off a candle.

"What's so unusual about your story," explained Justin, "is that it may have something to do with this altar I found in the ruins at River City. You see, each side is for a different element, for a total of seven, correct? Well, for starters, just two days ago, there were only six sides. The seventh, which appears to be in place for fire, just sprung up overnight, quite literally. I woke up, and there it was."

"That's admittedly a little strange, but how does this have anything to do with us?" inquired Stephen.

"Well, here, I need to get out my map." He reached under the cot and pulled out a rolled sheet of parchment, weathered slightly at the edges and yellowing with age. Unrolling it on the top of the altar, Justin made sure to be careful to not apply too much pressure, lest it crack and be ruined forever. The runes on the map, obviously labeling landmarks, were unknown to the three; Stephen, however, had the strangest feeling that he knew what they meant. The landmarks themselves, apart from being in some unusual art form, were quite apparent in nature.

"Here," said Justin, thrusting his finger at a point that looked like a large city. "This is Monsoon City. These cliffs to the East," he allowed his finger to slide to the right, "are what are known as the cliffs of Chevron. At their apex is one of the largest trees in the world, known as the Tree of Wind."

Angelo stood there with a look of annoyance on his face. "Is this why you think that what happened to us was interesting or unusual? Because the stupid tree is named the Tree of Wind!?"

"Calm yourself, youth; that's not the reason. Here, let me point some other things out; this here is the Lake on the Pillar. And this other unusually large tree, *the* largest one in the world, is the Tree of Life. Now here is the Castle of Eternal Spring. Anything familiar about any of these landmarks at all?"

Stephen saw the similarity immediately. "One of the runes describing each of the landmarks is the exact same symbol on each of the sides of this altar!"

"Exactly! Now, where is the final and most recent rune?"

It took everyone a while to find this one; John and Angelo had trouble telling all the different runes apart. Again, Stephen was the first to find it. "Here! At this volcano!"

"Yes; well, the map runes call it Fire Mountain, but they also label a castle on top of the volcano called Feuerschloss. Now, before two days ago, the castle was labeled, but didn't have this rune by it." He pointed out the telltale rune in case John and Angelo hadn't found it yet.

"And this is important, why?" inquired John.

"This is the thing: each of these runes corresponds to a different element, and the element of fire is the most recently acquired, apparently. Each of these runes also appears on the map at a landmark that obviously is named for the particular element. It just so happens that the temples of the Revered are located in the vicinity of each of these points."

John was most definitely and obviously confused, as were Angelo and Stephen. John was the one to ask the burning question present in everyone's head. "Just who exactly are these Revered?"

Justin had a blank look of disbelief upon his face. "You all mean to tell me that you've not even heard of the Revered?"

"If we had," stated Stephen, "we wouldn't have to ask, now, would we?"

"Of course not, that would be just stupid. Such logic must be why you are such a great wizard!" Stephen hung his head in embarrassment and disbelief. He didn't bother to retort. "Alright, as a brief overview, the Revered are a group of until this point six wizards who are so powerful and skilled with a certain kind of elemental magic that they have been entrusted with complete control of it. It is said that no man or woman who was not a member has ever laid eyes on them."

"And what does this have to do with us?" asked Angelo.

"I'm getting to that! Now, the new rune appeared yesterday morning, or quite possibly the night before. When I'm asleep, I tend not to notice things around me. Anyway, the very next morning, around eleven based on your departure time, your plane travels by the Tree of Wind and the Cliffs of Chevron, a part of the world where the Revered of Wind, Chevron, has the most control of atmospheric disturbances."

"So what are you saying?" asked John, trying to pull away from the possible conclusion.

"He's saying that our crash was no coincidence," deduced Stephen. "Whoever this Revered of Fire is, they have a sort of grudge on us, for some reason." Then, he had an idea, a slight inkling of a possibility. "Wait! Springsboro was destroyed by fire! Perhaps, because we lived, there is an intense hatred towards us! Our threat hails from Feuerschloss!"

John fidgeted slightly. Angelo noticed it, but said nothing.

"Well, if that is indeed the case, Feuerschloss is obviously quite a distance away," noted Justin, "so we must prepare for such a long journey. As I said before, I do have money, so supplies shouldn't be a problem. I see everyone here has a weapon; I do as well. My staff never leaves my side, and shall be used to your assistance. All I ask in return is the help of Stephen, to teach me the ways of the true wizard."

Stephen really didn't know what to do about this. He had no magical talent whatsoever. True, he had once dreamed of becoming a wizard, but that was a long time ago; he'd learned that it was not possible when he was young. To agree to this was to agree to a flat-out lie. They were out of money, however, and therefore out of any real options. He hated to do this, but there was no choice if they desired to continue. "I'll see what I can do."

Though Angelo was worried about how Stephen would repay such kindness, he breathed a sigh of relief that he would be able to sleep in a shelter that night and have the chance for more knowledge in the future. He was somewhat proud of Stephen's decision, and his facial expression betrayed his stoicism ever so slightly.

"Just one question," said John. "Can we sleep down here for the night?"

"Of course. I don't mind a little company; besides, upstairs is a little, well . . . let's not even discuss the upstairs."

*　　*　　*

Asmodeious hadn't been observing; he had been so infuriated by their survival that he went into the bowels of the castle and just lurked for hours on end. It was a way he got out frustration; just to know that he existed somewhere, and that his presence was felt if not seen, was a great sedative for his immense rage. It's not that he didn't want to go out and kill something; it was more that he didn't want to waste the energy doing so at this point. He would need all the energy he could muster, it would seem.

Diablo, on the other hand, had been watching the scene unfold through the cauldron. His actions hadn't deterred the group; if anything, the event had pointed the way. They knew where to go because of a stroke of luck that they walked into the cabana where that Justin character just happened to be. If they had just gone on into town, there would never have been this problem. Had they not lived, this would never have been a problem, either. *Why did my plans have to backfire?*, he asked himself. *They were perfect; we could have succeeded.* He wasn't angry; he was depressed and scared. He was also glad that Asmodeious had been downstairs. Had he seen this, everything would have been over. That was just his way.

11

Angelo's Introspection

They are dead. You know they're dead. You embraced the crumbling, blackened remains of their skeletons where you found them in the middle of that decimation you used to call your hometown. You held their disintegrating bodies one last time, tears running down your cheek, carving channels in their carbonized flesh. Gone. No bringing them back. So why are you on this insane quest? Revenge? You're certainly not going to save them with that.

Though, perhaps I couldn't be completely blamed; it was Justin who suggested this possibility of purposeful destruction. Justin . . . I have only just met him and already he's trying to wedge himself into the group. Were it not for our dire circumstances—"We need a room for the night, and we don't have any more money. Perhaps he could help us there," my exact words—we'd not have even been lying in this dungeon of a basement. The walls of fading gray trap the musty rotten smell of old parchment in the stale air, not entirely unpleasant, but it's unusual enough to be disheartening. No, we wouldn't even have paid any heed to him; we would have left him in front of that beach cabana, rambling on about how Stephen was supposed to help him or some nonsense. How was Stephen supposed to help *anyone* with magic? I remember this one time, when the street-performing magician came to town and he kept botching all his tricks whenever Stephen was around. Yeah, like he could help anyone along that vein.

Even this Justin figure's *house* is a lie; sure, we're staying in the concrete bunker underground, but we had seen what he passed off as his real living quarters. I should have known nothing could possibly live in such squalor.

No wonder the magic community hates his guts; he's probably lied about a lot more things.

So why did you trust him enough to follow him to his house? Why do you trust what he says about the fire? It puts a face on their deaths, that's why. You know it's why. Admit it; you find comfort in the thought that your parents died on purpose. Oh, isn't that it? Then what is that moisture running down your left cheek as you clench your eyes shut, trying to shut out the world and shut up your thoughts, inevitably spiraling towards the truth you know to be real—this trek has no purpose.

We're going to get to Feuerschloss—if that's even where this perpetrator is, though it fits both what Justin claimed and Stephen and I witnessed—we're going to kill whatever tenants we found, and it will be glorious and bloody. We'd be just like them; killing without purpose, without reason, without logic. There certainly wasn't any logic behind what had happened.

Why am I on this journey? Why couldn't I have just stayed in Chartreuse or Topaz, wiling away the years as an old hermit, never speaking to people again? I wouldn't have to kill. There'd be no need for revenge. I'd be secluded, forgetting and repressing all that I had seen—it was just two days ago, wasn't it?—happily ever after. I could have lived with myself then—not a murderer, not a warrior, just a simple man with simple ways, living out the rest of his long, long life.

Remember what happened that morning? You were so excited at even the prospect of spending the day hunting with Stephen; you wanted so badly to try out your new longsword, to show off for him. So you woke up extra early, got ready, and ran down to his house as fast as you could. He was still asleep, or so you reasoned when he didn't come to the door. That's right, you broke his window trying to wake him up; you threw that odd rock just a little too hard. Woke him up, though. Heh, you didn't even hardly care that you did it, so long as he was willing to go. And he was; oh, when you heard him agree how your heart leaped in your chest at the anticipation, the excitement. You would have had that buck, too, had it not been frightened away by whatever is was . . .

At least John had been willing to help out, for whatever reason—it couldn't have been hometown loyalty, since he so readily shed that when he moved to set up a shop. Did he only do it out of duty to family? Why am I looking for excuses to hate him so much? Why can't I trust him? John had the sense, the initiative to start his own business when his parents passed away. He was intelligent enough to set up shop in a larger town. His network of trade for various merchandise and subsequent knowledge made him the best-suited man for this kind of journey. He's *Stephen's brother*, for goodness sake. *What more do you need? Just because he's human, you want to distance yourself? Stephen's just as human as he is. You yourself have a human fathe-err, had. Go ahead, sob quietly into your arms; that way if John ever notices or finds out, he can just humiliate you.*

Then there was the plane crash. We had really lucked out there, surviving that. What's more, we happened to wash up on just the shore we had been trying to get to in the first place. It even helped Justin formulate a possible explanation for what had been happening, when we ran into him at the cabana. *You have trouble trusting even him, don't you?* He's full-blooded elf, yet doesn't seem to have any connection whatsoever with nature. Well, I guess that's not true; he did say he knew of Stephen from his dreams, so that's at least *some* connection, odd as it is. But then, there's the complete lie of a lifestyle he's living; that lowers his reputation in my eyes.

This bunker, while not exactly clean, was definitely more-so than upstairs. The large stone altar in the center of the room Justin "liberated" from the ruins of River City stands stoically; it seems highly unlikely something that obviously solid would suddenly morph another facet, but Justin insists that's what happened, and what gave him the idea that something destroyed our town on purpose, hailing from that castle. The map of the world, displaying the same markings as the altar, was probably still laying atop it; the one thing that strung together Justin's story continuously, that map is what convinced Stephen that Justin might be on to something.

What's that sound? Oh, just Stephen snoring. Glad he's at least getting some sleep. Then again, it's not like he lost anyone in the fire—you were both out hunting, so he didn't lose you, and his brother had set up shop in Chartreuse many years ago when their parents died. So, what was his purpose? Why was he joining you on this quest? It certainly wasn't for revenge. Did he know more than he led on? It wouldn't be unlike him; he always did seem to know more about any given situation than he should have. But what *does he know? Does he know that he knows? Does he realize his complete comfort and acceptance of this whole thing makes you uneasy? Fearful, even?*

Fearful? Yes, I hadn't noticed it before, but it's true—I'm afraid of him. Afraid of his calm, his nonchalance, his cold calculating acknowledgment of everything that was going on. I'd known him since his early childhood, and never before have I imagined he'd ever become like this. Has he matured? Is this what happens when you grow up?

Maybe that's my purpose—I want to get myself killed so I wouldn't grow up to be like that. But, then again, what if that calm comfort is a good thing? *What if it helps you realize your full potential against this enemy? Heh, there you go again about the enemy.* I don't even know what this enemy is, yet I'm scared shitless of it. Though, it did bring ruin upon a town in a matter of seconds. I have every right to be afraid of it. If, that is, it's what killed my parents.

There's no doubt in your mind anymore, is there. It definitely did it. True, they were just bystanders as far as whatever that . . . thing *was was concerned, but they're dead now as a result. And you cowered under a hollow tree until it passed over again. You coward.* That's *why you're on this quest—you want to prove you're not a pissant. Sure, you've got your sword—you're quite the big man with your sword, aren't you? You know what happens to the coward in these stories, right? They die. You are going to die. You're going to be scared as hell, turn your back to run away, and be struck down where you stand. Oh God. You shouldn't be here. You should leave. Now. Before you hinder this. Go. Your fear is only going to—*

"Angelo." *Stephen. But, he's asleep, isn't he?* "Angelo, calm down . . . shh . . ."

"How can you expect me to calm down? They *died*, Stephen! I'm afraid . . . afraid of what that thing is going to do to me!" The meager sheets are my only comfort as I squeeze the hell out of them, tears collecting again.

"Shh, don't worry about it. It's perfectly fine to be scared. I know I put on a big-man face of fearlessness and bravery, but that's just a mask. To be honest, I'm just as afraid of this as you are."

The snot running down my nose is just uncomfortable enough to make me sniff it back in; *that's just sick.* " . . . Really?"

"Really. And you don't think Justin or John are frightened, either? Look at them! Justin's a bloody chicken; that much is obvious from the facade put on upstairs with the mangled mendacity of a house. And seriously, wouldn't I know my own brother?"

"Maybe you do, but I—"

"Trust me on this, Angelo. The guy's a scaredy-cat."

It was hard to imagine John being afraid of anything; he was such a . . . he seemed like such a bully. The image of him running away from anything—*go ahead and chuckle; it's funny.* "But then how will we—"

"Shh, don't worry about that now. We'll do it, and it'll be spectacular. Justin said he's going to help us do research, remember? We'll find a way, most definitely."

"Stephen . . ."

"Yes?"

" . . . thank you."

"Don't worry about it. Now get some sleep; we've got a long journey ahead of us, and you'll need your strength."

Sleep. Yes, that sounds like a good idea . . .

12

John's Introspection

God damn mother-fucking son of a bitch, how the hell did this happen? How the fuck did you get caught up in this shit? On the one hand, you have to ki—keep an eye on your brother; on the other, you feel like . . . almost like all this was your fault. Now, you've flat-out lied to your only brother's face, led on his best friend, and gotten a completely random stranger involved in a quest that, had it been anyone else, you'd have no problem following through with. How exactly will you get yourself out of this one?

Thank god Justin came in when he did, though; otherwise, I'd be the one blamed for all this in the end. With a new face on the quest, mistrust will be diverted away from me and I'll finally be able to relax a bit and focus myself on figuring out what ending I want to witness. In the end, I know . . . I'm going to kill something. Somehow, by my hand, one of these figures surrounding me literally and figuratively will die.

Maybe I should just kill Justin and run off. That fucker figured out exactly what happened from just a few minuscule verbal hints, and then had the gall to actually tell us. True, there was a part of me that knew Asmodeious had destroyed Springsboro and set them on their quest, but I didn't want to *hear* it, dammit! He was so damn *quick*, too! Someone that smart miraculously stumbles upon each piece of information necessary to come to the correct conclusion; it's just not normal.

Oh god, has he figured out what happened regarding you? Does he know why you're here? Look at him, sleeping all comfortably on his cot without a care in the world. That smug bastard, he already fucking figured it out! He knows you're in regular contact with the one they're all trying to destroy; he knows you're the pawn!

Fuck that; I'm no one's pawn. I chose to join with him of my own free will. True, the choices were to aid him or be destroyed, but I find anyone can be bought with the correct bargain. Besides, he did mention a reward. Fuck! How the hell can I even think of the reward when it involves . . . no! I'll observe; that's all he asks now anyway.

Dear lord, he's going to tear me a new one when he finds out what happened though, if he hasn't already discovered. This shit is going to be painful, I just know it.

Why the hell are you punishing yourself for this? You make yourself more suspicious by drawing attention to yourself, yelling and carrying on like you do. I just don't want them to find out; I couldn't live with myself. *Then why? Why do you do it?* Because . . .

Because I fear for my life, that's why. I'm deathly afraid he's going to somehow reach through that mirror of his and rip my heart out, drinking the blood as it flows from the weakly-pumping arteries, all the while smiling that sadistic, sarcastic smirk, never removing his yellow gaze from mine. *You brought this on yourself,* his eyes would say, and mine would close, sealing my fate as my head nods forward. The very thought makes me shudder.

All you have to do to remove yourself from that demise is sacrifice one of them first, you know. That's all it takes. Angelo's blade rests against the altar; all you'd have to do is reach out, cut someone's throat, and it'd be over. Sure, you'd have to run to avoid being caught by the others, but Asmodeious wouldn't be on your ass any more. You'd be safe.

It's not like it was my fault to begin with; had the mirror never entered Chartreuse, I wouldn't have this dilemma on my hands. The traveling merchant who sold it to me even told me there was an ancient rumor of a curse on it, but we laughed it off together. Cheap-ass traveling merchants.

That evening, you could have just as easily ignored the calls from the mirror, too. No, you had to investigate; you had to see who had somehow sneaked into your house.

Evil. Pure, unadulterated evil. That's what my eyes met that night. Oh, that the demon of memory were not strangling me, that I could cast off the hatred I gazed upon as I rounded the corner, finding the mirror a frame for that sinister portrait. Any man would fear; he who wouldn't is no mortal of this world, that's for certain. The visage that glared back from that accursed implement . . .

That's right; anyone in your situation would have done the same, wouldn't they? Everyone acts big, but they're all fucking cowards at heart. Hell, they wouldn't even be debating like this, would they? They'd roll over, doing exactly what Asmodeious wants.

But, isn't that what I'm—

"John."

Is that . . . Stephen? Oh shit! Shit shit shit! He's on to me! "Stephen! It's not what you think! I don't want to—"

"John, I don't care."

Blink. Did he just say . . . "You don't care?"

"Of course not." He's coming closer! What do I do? Did he hear me talking to myself? "I'm not you. I cannot tell you how to live your life; that's your responsibility. What you want in life is none of my business."

I can't look away from his eyes, those portals that must be gazing into my soul and judging me every second. *You're shivering; he'll definitely know something's up!* "But . . . Steve, you might . . . I might—"

"And that was my choice. If you remember, you chose to come with us. You're absolutely allowed to stop here if you'd prefer." Wait . . . "You don't have to accompany us all the way; that's not your responsibility."

Does he think . . . He has no clue! He hasn't noticed anything! I sigh internally, my relief surely showing on my face. "Stephen, you know I can't do that. I have every bit as much responsibility to those who died as you do."

His pat on my back is clearly misplaced, but what he doesn't know won't hurt him yet. "If that's how you feel, I won't stop you; neither will I judge you if you decide to stay."

"No, but your friend will." Not like I care what he thinks at this point, really; if Steve doesn't suspect a thing, there was no way that idiot half-elf could.

"True, but that's just his nature; he doesn't like opening up to people he doesn't know, and he doesn't know you like I do." *Which is exactly why he won't be a problem.* "Don't worry about that now though. Just let us know in the morning if you want to stay here. Either way, use this wonderful situation we've found ourselves in to get some sleep in the meantime."

Indeed, I've been worrying myself too much lately to get much sleep; my brother's clear naiveté has lifted much of that weight from me. "Sleep . . . that sounds like a good idea right now. Thanks for the advise, my brother."

"Don't mention it."

13

Justin's Introspection

He's here! He's really here! Oh happy day, that you happened to be in the cabana at just the right time; you might not have crossed paths otherwise! Of course, that's foolish; we were destined to meet at some point. Still, how wonderful that it happened so quickly! I'll have to ask him about all sorts of things . . . but in due time. He's tired clearly, and who could blame him? The plane crash his party had been in would have brought even the strongest man to exhaustion. Unfortunate, that . . . the plane crash, I mean. Sure, it brought him to me more immediately, but did it really have to result with a death?

And then there's the original matter, the whole reason he even came here to begin with—the matter of Springsboro. Such a tiny town it must have been, that you've never heard of it; its name implies governance of either Manas or Dryad, but that could put it anywhere really. Near Topaz City, at any rate; that one you have heard of, but you've never been there. Meant to a long time ago, when you first had visions of him. Well, really it was more that he had visions of me, wasn't it? I mean, they were his dreams; I just happened to be in them. Such a strong sorcerer, to be able to accomplish such in his sleep!

You've circumnavigated the problem at hand, as usual. This is exactly why you'll never amount to anything; your thought processes are just too tangential! Springsboro was burned to the ground. An entire village destroyed, in either Revered's dominion? Such was indeed highly suspect. Surely one of them had noticed? Shouldn't they have requested Miranda's aid in extinguishing the flames? Or would they have possibly . . . No! How could I think so selfishly! They wouldn't have let an entire village be destroyed just to bring me a tutor. Such would be immoral! Impossible for those benevolent masters of nature.

But then, why *did* they allow this to happen? What was this new Revered of Fire up to? His appearance wasn't until after the fire, if the group's story was to be believed. Was he the one who razed the town? Or was there another, lurking backstage, waiting for the right moment to engulf the rest of us in his death-flame?

You'll figure this out. In spite of your wandering thoughts, you do have a knack for connecting the dots. After all, with all the evidence you presented a hypothesis Stephen himself came to on his own; you just can't condemn skill like that!

Speaking of evidence, what a marvelous trip that had been; I regularly spend much time in the ruins of River City hoping to glean some insight or knowledge from the ancient crumbling halls therein, but never did I imagine I'd encounter the altar. Clearly neither did its previous user, as it was well-hidden in a back room of a building remnant on the very outskirts of the city. What might the purpose of such a thing have been? Clearly candles had been important in its use, but what else transpired on its surface in days long gone? Why was such a thing thought necessary? The truly phenomenal thing about it, of course, was the map. I just happened upon it in a traveling merchant's refuse; he wanted to dispose of several parchments, and apparently felt the map was of similar value. Oh, how little he knew! *Yes, you recognized the runes immediately; true, you had been in possession of the altar for some time, but that only made the appearance of the runes that much more surprising!*

Of course, if I were truly all that brilliant, I probably wouldn't require Stephen's assistance. He claims he knows no magic, but how can that be? Is he actually unaware of his own power? *If that's true, how could he even hope to begin to help you? He'd be in the same boat you are! No, that can't be. He's far too powerful to not realize how powerful he is. His dreams are proof of that!*

Speaking of which, is he asleep presently? Yes, you saw him drift off first of all the group, remember? You even made a joke about how the day must have really worn on him, and—what was his name, Angelo? Angelo, yes, he shot daggers at you with his eyes for that. You'll have to be more careful around this group if you wish to obtain the assistance you so desperately require.

Wait, is that . . . Stephen? Why is he awa—no! He must be dreaming again! Am I asleep? That's the only sensible conclusion; he was clearly wiped out not . . . how long ago was it? Sleep is so confusing when it comes to time. Surely no more than two hours ago. Two?

"Why do the Revered hate us so much? Do they just want tribute or something? Asses."

What? Why did he think—no! That's not right; the Revered are incapable of hate! Besides, they would never demand tribute; they just aren't like that!

"Aren't like what?" Oh dear; did I say that out loud? Crap, he's turning around! What do I do? "What are you doing here? Aren't you supposed to be asleep?"

Is this another test? "Stephen, I am asleep; you—" No; if he doesn't realize it, then maybe it's best like that. " . . . Never mind. The Revered aren't the conceited beings you just surmised them to be. I know."

"How can you know? If what we concluded earlier was in fact the truth, they're directly responsible for everything so far! They killed Dave!" Dave? Was he the pilot of their plane?

"Stephen, you've got it all wrong; the Revered only act in the interest of the land; they would never go out of their way to perform such heinous acts! Certainly, everything so far indicates they're involved; however, they just can't be the primary cause."

"Why not? Because they're these ultimate wizards? You think the same thing of me; could I not just reach for Amoras and slit your throat right this moment?"

"Stephen, you're—" You're using a straw man argument! It's illogical! *No; he's only acting emotionally. He's stressed and he's scared. Anyone would be after the past few days he's had. A hometown destroyed, a best friend grieving the loss of his parents, and a sudden possibly-forced plane crash . . .* What a fool I've been. I should give him his space; let him calm down and collect his thoughts before bugging him again about assistance. I'm so sorry. "The Revered are simply incapable of such things! It's not in their nature."

"Nature? Seeing as I've never met these so-called Revered, I can make no judgment on their nature until I encounter it with my own eyes. I simply cannot trust you on this right now."

"Why not? I've studied the Revered since I was a child; as a wizard myself, I had to! It was part of the standard curriculum. I'm the only member of your party that knows as much as I do about them; why can I not be trusted on this?"

And suddenly we were above-ground, in what I had called my home before. Stephen had transported us with the mere flourish of a hand! "Because of this, Justin. Look around you; look at this lie you live! This was the first thing we found out about you, and all we know about you so far has been based on this massive, unwieldy lie! Not once have we heard anything from you that might be construed as absolute truth. How do I know you're even a wizard? You claim to be of the clan of Bailey, but how do I know that's not a lie too? You want to learn to be a better sorcerer? Start by being a better person and just being truthful!"

Ouch. Such a bitter first lesson. Was I really so despicable, that everything I said was suspect? I hadn't lied to them once! Everything I'd told them was the truth! Every ounce of it! "Do you really hate me so much, that you'd distrust everything I say?"

"Did I say I hated you? I just don't know you. Looks do not form a good judge of character, but actions speak volumes. You're obviously learned, or at least very good at portraying such; however, I cannot trust your word blindly until I begin to see some sort of repentance for these non-truths."

Indeed; you've got a lot to learn. "Stephen, I—I'm sorry . . ."

"No. Not in words. Action. Show me that you can be trusted. But tomorrow, not right now. It's very late, and we've got a long journey ahead of us."

"Yes, you're right. Sleep is most important right now." And yet, how little he clearly knows of his own situation. I leave him for now, anyway; he really does need his space, especially after all my doting on him.

A better person by being more—no, just flat-out truthful. But how can I do that? My very place in society is held together by this lie I live!

But that's exactly what he means. You know as well as he that, if you were truthful about everything, you might just develop the discipline you so lack, that very discipline you masquerade as having.

Does everyone in this group feel the same way about me? Surely they must; what a fool I've been! Not only do none of them trust me, but none of them thinks I'm even cut out to be a wizard, I'm certain. Well, I'll just have to change that!

Change? You mean you're actually going to shape up? No more leisurely strolls to the cabana, no more reading about history without doing anything to contribute yourself?

Well, nobody said anything about refusing to take a break every once in a while. Besides, the folks at the cabana would surely miss me. No, maybe not a drastic sudden change, but a change must begin to happen. And I must be at the center of that change, I think.

You think? There you go being all wishy-washy again.

No. I know. I resolve from here on out to change my duplicitous ways, and to do everything in my power to become a better person, for my sake and for this quest's. After all, didn't I tell Stephen myself? I'm the most knowledgeable individual in their group now, at least with regards to the Revered. And indeed, they're involved in all this somehow.

Tomorrow's going to be a big day, I just know it. Maybe that sleep isn't such a bad idea after all.

14

Stephen's Introspection

What I wouldn't give for a blanket right now; I had no idea stone could be so cold a surface as to sap the very heat from a body. Heck, even a thick coat would help. Jeans and a t-shirt are not optimal coverings for this kind of experience. A pillow would be nice too, but I suppose that's a luxury we're all going to have to do without. That plane crash completely wiped out the majority of our inventory, leaving us with whatever happened to be on us at the time. We're lucky to even have weapons after that.

Poor Dave, dying for a cause he could not have known. He probably lies at the bottom of the ocean with his plane at this point, an unwilling, unknowing sacrifice to aid your haste. Indeed, he fought valiantly against that microburst, struggling with all his might to keep the craft under control; were it not for his efforts, you all would likely have joined him in death.

What about his family? Did he have any surviving relatives? What will they think? Will they ever even hear about his demise, or will they go about their lives, completely ignorant of the events that led to his loss? When he doesn't return, will they think to scour the sea for him? If they find his corpse, will they take note of the distinct lack of passengers in his vehicle? So many unknowns, most of them left for others to postulate. I pity them.

Why are we even on this quest? Because our town was burned to the ground? Angelo has a cause, certainly; what is mine? What is John's, for that matter? I mean, we've already been the direct cause of one death more than necessary, if Justin's hypothesis is correct—and why shouldn't it be? *It makes perfect sense; hell, you came to the same conclusion before he even said anything.* My head hurts. Dammit, this floor is cold! Ugh, best not to think about it too much I suppose. Certainly, the sheer volume of deceased after the past few days is cause enough besides.

What am I going to do about Justin, though? The man thinks I'm worthy of worship practically; why? What have I done to earn that? He seems to believe I have some sort of magical ability. I know for a fact that I don't; I'm just a normal guy. Aren't I? I mean, aside from this quest, aside from losing my hometown to a mysterious fire caused by an equally-mysterious force. Why do these Revered hate us so much? Is it because we don't know them enough to pay them homage? What a bunch of asses, if that's the case.

"No." Behind me; Justin? "They aren't like that; I just know it."

"Aren't like what? Why are you here? Aren't you supposed to be asleep?"

"I am asleep, Stephen; you're . . . never mind, that's not important. The Revered are not the stuck-up individuals you just concluded, I'm sure of it."

"How can you be so sure? If what you said is correct, they're the direct cause of all this! They're the ones that burned our village to the ground! They killed Dave!"

"No. Stephen, the Revered act merely in the interest of the land; they do not go out of their way to do such things! Certainly, everything seems to indicate they are involved; however, they themselves are not the direct cause."

"Why not? Because they're the supreme mages? You proclaim that I'm a supreme mage too; am I incapable of such acts? Could I not just slit your throat right here and now?"

"Stephen, it's not like that! The Revered . . . they can't! It's simply not in their nature!"

"Well, I know nothing of their nature; I suppose I'll just have to judge when next we encounter this force that's out to kill us. Unfortunately, I can't just trust your word in this."

"Why not? I've studied the Revered since I was a child; as a wizard myself, I had to! I didn't have a choice. I'm the only member of your party that knows as much as I do about them; why can I not be trusted on this?"

"Because, Justin." I motioned around us, the background lighting up to reveal Justin's upstairs quarters, his front the rest of the world knew. The crumbling walls, the strand-board table, the shattered glassware, all testaments to the falsehood that was Justin's image. "Because of this.

Everything we've seen of you so far has been a lie! Not once have you told us the truth about yourself. How do I know you're even a wizard? You claim to be of the class of Bailey, but how do I know that's not a lie too? You want to learn to be a better sorcerer? Start by being a better person and just being truthful!"

Justin cringed visibly. "Do you hate me so much for that, that you'd completely distrust anything I say?"

"Did I say I hated you?" *Sigh.* "I just don't know you. Looks do not form a good judge of character, but actions speak volumes. You're obviously learned, or at least very good at portraying such; however, I cannot trust your word blindly until I begin to see some sort of repentance for these non-truths."

"Stephen, I—I'm sorry . . ."

"No. Not in words. Action. Show me that you can be trusted. But tomorrow, not right now. It's very late, and we've got a long journey ahead of us."

"Yes, you're right. Sleep is most important right now." Justin leaves my presence, head hung. As he retreats to his cot, a faint muttering graces my ears; I focus on finding it, eyes meeting the cowering figure of my own brother, curled up around a rather fancy-looking garment. Upon closer inspection . . . *That's the same thing he was wearing in that dream from before!* No matter; clearly, something about it is upsetting him. "John."

He looks up at me, a wild panic in his eyes. "Stephen! It's not what you think—I'm not—"

"John, I don't care."

He cocks his head, obviously thrown off by my response. "You . . . don't care?"

"Of course not." I walk over to him, kneeling to have a look at the cloak. "I'm not you, and I cannot tell you how to live your life. It's none of my business what you want."

He keeps eye contact, something I didn't expect; something had truly shaken him to the core. "Steve . . . but . . . you could end up—"

"So? That was my choice. And it was yours to follow us. You can stop now, if you want. You don't have to join us if you really don't want to; it's not your responsibility."

His expression softens immensely. "Steve, you know I can't do that. I have just as much responsibility to this quest as you do, and you know that."

I give a light chuckle and pat him on the back firmly. "If you say so, bud. It's up to you; I won't judge you if you stay here."

"No, but that jerk half-elf friend of yours will." He grins, obviously playing around now.

"Indeed, Angelo's not the kind to open up to others very easily; he just doesn't know you like I do. But don't worry about it; now is not the time to contemplate. If you want to stay, just tell us tomorrow; either way, take advantage of this shelter while we can and get some sleep."

"Sleep . . ." He yawns, the gaudy garment falling to the ground. "Yes, that sounds like a plan. Thanks, Steve."

"No problem." He flops down and passes out right then and there.

Suddenly, to my right . . . whimpering? I turn to look, and am transported to Springsboro. The sight is infinitely worse than I remembered; a pile of corpses towering to the reddened sky rests in the town square, bodies contorted in sheer horror, all completely carbonized. At the disgusting mountain's base, a lone child kneels, cradling the remains of two people in his arms. I recognize him immediately; I'd be a poor friend to not. "Angelo."

He turns to face me, his visage soaked with tears, mouth open in a gaping sob. I can't help but run forward and embrace the pitiful child tightly, stroking his soft hair. "Shh, it's okay, you're okay . . ."

"Oh, Stephen!" He chokes back a sob, his little arms squeezing my midsection desperately. "They're dead . . . why are they dead!? I'm so scared, that thing . . ."

"Oh, Angelo . . ." I continue embracing him, rubbing his back in an attempt to comfort him. "It's okay to be scared. I am, too; I don't know what's going to happen to us, and it scares me half to death."

He sniffles, wiping his nose on his sleeve as he looks up at me. "Really?"

I nod and smile at him. "Of course I am, and I'm not the only one. Look at Justin and John." I point out the two sleeping companions. "They're absolutely terrified! Justin obviously is; hell, he's scared even of the people he knows, it seems. He wouldn't hide his true self from the world like he does otherwise. And John, well, he's my brother; I should know."

Angelo looks at the two others, his tears having stopped. "But, John doesn't seem so scared to me . . ."

"Trust me, he's terrified."

The child giggles at the thought. It comforts me to see him do that. "But, what about this?" He looks back at the pile of burned cadavers. "How will we—"

"Don't worry about that right now. We'll figure out how to do it, and it will be spectacular. Justin's going to help us, and together we'll all stop whatever it is, absolutely."

He turns back to look at me, smiling. Before my eyes, he matures, resuming his current age. "Stephen . . ."

"Yes?"

"Thank you so much."

"Don't worry about it. Now get some sleep; we've got a long journey ahead of us, and you'll need your strength."

He nods and turns away, disappearing again.

That's why you need to go; everyone else needs you. This group couldn't make it without guidance. I nod, lying back down. Indeed, they all seem to need a common thread; if that's all I am to the party, so be it. I'm willing to stick around just for that, if only because it's at least a purpose. My eyes close, and I drift off to sleep finally.

The floor really is quite cold.

15

Coterie

It was the second morning in a row either Angelo, Stephen, or John had woken up without sunlight; not one of them was any more used to it. This time however, Justin was there to assist, meaning they could pack up and get on the road far earlier than the previous day allowed. Indeed, Justin seemed the most rested of the four, and though he did wait until everyone was awake before packing, he was still the one waiting for everyone else. Both Does were bleary-eyed; of course, none of the three former Springsboro denizens actually had anything to prepare outside their armor and weapons, but this was still time-consuming for all of them. Eventually, the entire troop was prepared for departure; Justin, being the owner of the land, went up to ground level first to assist the others.

"You know Justin," began Stephen as they embarked, "last night I was too tired to take notice of our surroundings; I know we walked for some time, but where exactly are we?" He surveyed the small dirt path they were walking down; "I mean, not to belittle anyone or anything, but this seems like a relatively poor part of town, in spite of the large land plots."

Short chicken-wire fences delimited, as Stephen had observed, rather unusually large pieces of land along the minor venue; however, every house in sight was similar in construction to Justin's own, though perhaps in a better condition. Shacks really better described what these structures were, and to assume any had even what the three might have considered basic amenities was stretching the limits of imagination perhaps just a bit too far.

"Well, there's a bit of history behind that; would you care to hear it?"

John and Angelo both rolled their eyes; they knew they were in for a long hike of excessive discourse between the history geek and the local. Stephen reacted as expected—with over-exuberant glee. "Would I ever!"

Justin cleared his throat and began his exposition. "This is Flood City's East District, and indeed it's one of the poorest parts of the city; land value here has been incredibly low for—well, for as long as history has seen fit to record it. You see—you know why it's called Flood City, correct?"

John piped up to answer, wanting to be able to get a word in himself. "Because every year the runoff from the regular monsoons in Monsoon City causes the region to flood. Could we—"

"Exactly! But what causes the monsoons? There's a regular air current that actually brings water from Sapphire Ocean up to Monsoon City where, when it gets warm enough during the early summer for the current to move far enough north, yet still cool enough for the moisture to only be lifted so high into the atmosphere, the waters condense because of the sudden pressure increase upon colliding with the Cliffs of Chevron. Thus an excess of rain falls upon the region, causing a large amount of flooding here in Flood City once it actually gets back down here. For the record, Miranda, the Revered of water, was the first to explain this phenomenon."

"That's fascinating!" Stephen was clearly overjoyed that someone was catering to his desire for knowledge, barely taking notice as the fences began thinning out, the four leaving the northern bounds of Flood City. "But, what does that have to do with this?"

"You see, the Cliffs of Chevron are actually quite rich in nutrients important in farming; this is why Monsoon City has thrived, because these nutrients are brought out of the rock as a result of the rains and deposited in their soil. However, by the time the waters first get to Flood City, they have no further nutrients in them. The result is that it strips away any topsoil in the Eastern District. Because the floodwaters rarely get high enough to cover that part of the city, the soil is gone for good. This land can't be farmed, is incredibly difficult to build a foundation in, and always gets washed out once a year. Therefore, there's little use for the land, and its value is low."

"A-ha! And that must be why the ancient Assimmians settled here; the silt build-up from this area would have surely made Flood City a bountiful harvest."

"That's exactly right! Or at least, that's what most historians believe; there's not much left of the old Assimmian civilization for any sort of data extrapolation. Of course, presently the farming districts to the south of the

City proper make a very successful harvest of rice every year, and enough livestock to feed everyone in city limits."

"Wait a minute." It was Angelo's turn to interject. "If the city floods every year, why does Cibola Beach still exist? That doesn't make any sense."

"Oh, didn't I explain that? Cibola Beach actually stretches south of Flood City. You see, the floodwaters that run off into the ocean are still fairly rich in silt; this deposits right off the coast, where it feeds a massive coral reef. Coincidentally, that's one of the big draws for many tourists. Anyway, many of the fish that subsequently feed off the abundance of coral and algae there produce the pristine white sands that make up the beach! It's all a beautiful coincidence that just happens to converge in the region of Flood City."

"Ah; I suppose that makes sense." Angelo nodded in understanding.

"So Justin," John wanted to change the subject of discussion to something more directly relevant to the present journey. "You said you had money, correct? And food? I didn't see you gather any such thing at your place, and I'd expect, had you kept such at your place, it might disappear at the hands of your neighbors while you're busy not being home. Where is this wealth of resources we will certainly require for the remainder of our travels?"

"Oh yes, I suppose I never did explicitly state that." Justin changed his subject matter immediately. "My money and food are all kept in my lab in Monsoon City; it's really my home away from home, only I spend more time there."

"Ah yes, now I remember; you mentioned something about that last night, correct?"

"Perhaps I did; I was too excited about the possibility of the circumstances surrounding your crash to really pay attention to what I was saying. At any rate, don't worry about it; Monsoon City is a mere day's journey from Flood City. We'll arrive at my lab shortly before sunset, by my reckoning."

"So what you're saying is, we don't have any food at all until this evening, when we'll be arriving in a city where everything will likely be closed anyway by the time we get there?" John stopped, arms crossed, tapping his foot in the dirt, clearly annoyed at this turn of events. "You didn't think this through very well, did you?"

Justin was caught off-guard by this attack of logic. "Err—well, you see—But, I do this all the time . . . oh, right! There are fruit trees along parts of the road; they'll be mature by this time of year. If you get hungry, you could just partake of one."

John shrugged in defeat. "Fruit isn't exactly what I had in mind, but food is food. You're sure it's free for the taking?"

"Oh, absolutely! The trail winds through the jungle; no one owns that land."

*   *   *

Miranda was not pleased. Pacing through her palace, she tried to make sense of what had transpired the previous morning. Of all parts of the world she made sure got regular precipitation, Monsoon City and Flood City were her two favorite locations because of the truly artful manner in which both received their rain. Though the monsoon season had just passed, the events of the previous morning were still distressing; it meant a delayed harvest for the region's farmers, and could very well push back the next year's rains by several weeks. This was truly troubling for the elf.

Why would he do that? She thought to herself. A burst that strong and that seemingly-random in direction could have only been an act of Chevron. What was the dwarf up to? He knew as well as she that the winds of the region needed to be left alone for the well-being of everyone who lived there.

Then of course, there was the matter of that plane. A small single-propeller aircraft, the kind Chevron himself favored because of its similarity to his own creation, had been blown so forcefully as to cause it to crash in the ocean. Had it not been for her quick observation and action, everyone on board would have died, not just the pilot. What was going on here? She decided to pay the corpulent windbag a visit, maybe shake some answers out of him.

Marching through the alabaster halls of her floating palace, Miranda brought herself to a specialized room; resembling a closet in size and structure, this was one of two transportation portals in her residence. This particular one was a direct link to the Roaming Edifice; as she stepped in, the elf found herself surrounded by the familiar water cascades, the freshwater scent, the cool touch of moisture that was her meditation chamber. The brickwork square upon which she now stood was the masterwork of Rhox, while the transportation spells had been crafted skillfully by Luna; every Revered had contributed to the construction of the Edifice in some way, save for their newest member. Miranda made a mental note to discuss with Salamandro the nature of his own meditation chamber and Edifice contributions.

She stepped out of the enclosed room and into the open hallway Diablo would have been more familiar with; floors of granite, grand white pillars, the hall opened out into a cloud-bank to the left, enclosed by further rooms to the right. This wall was constructed of sandstone, again Rhox's doing; he wanted to incorporate materials from all around the world, these stones being formed of the more solid parts of the Desert. He had to change compositions for the inside of her chamber, she recalled; water and sandstone didn't mix particularly well. Still, outside like this it was quite lovely, in her opinion.

Across the way, Miranda could make out the hallway she needed to be in; Chevron's chamber was the opposite direction from the throne room, in the middle of the hall. This might have been mildly troublesome were it not for her own contribution to the Edifice's construction; she stepped out into the open air, only to be supported seemingly by the very clouds themselves. Indeed, that was exactly what they were doing; Miranda had long ago enchanted these clouds, both binding them to the Edifice and coercing them to support whatever living weight happened to pass through them.

Miranda proceeded thusly through the sky, across to the opposite hall. Setting foot on solid rock again, she gave a silent thanks to the water and moved to Chevron's chamber. It had been some time since she had felt the need to set foot in the vertigo-inducing room, so she was mildly unprepared for the burst of hot air that greeted her face upon opening the door.

Within, she recalled exactly why she did not like this enclosure. Truly, to call it an enclosure was incorrect; there was no ceiling, and only the bare minimum floor kept its occupants aloft. Through this tunnel, forceful gales blew up and out, swirling around inside the restrictive walls. Miranda had to hold her hair back to keep it out of her face while simultaneously attempting to keep her robes from lifting as well. Seated in a pose of deep thought, Chevron floated in the center of the room. *What luck,* she thought; *I won't have to venture down and search his little tree fort for him.*

The dwarf, sensing the door having opened, peered through one eye at the intruder. "Oh, Miranda!" He dropped from his seated position onto the square beneath him, identical to the one in her own chamber. "I thought you didn't like this place. What brings you here at such an unusual hour?"

"Funny, that. And here I thought you liked Monsoon City, too."

Chevron was visibly taken aback by this comment. "What do you mean? Nothing's happened to them, has it?"

"Not yet, you lummox, but thanks to your actions yesterday I'm going to be scrambling to make sure they can produce a decent harvest next year!

What the hell were you thinking, a microburst? *Away* from your cliffs? What possessed you to do something so foolish?"

Chevron winced with every new question, each its own verbal assault on his very character. "Miranda, calm down; it's not like this is something I do all the time! That plane—"

"And that's another thing! You brought down a plane in your stupidity! One person died as a direct result of your actions; had I not intervened, three others would have befallen the same fate!"

"You *saved* them!? What the hell, Miranda; those people were plotting to destroy us!"

Miranda stopped herself, panting from the exertion of yelling at the dwarf. "Plotting to destroy us? That's a heavy charge there, Chevron; what makes you think this?"

"Salamandro informed me of it that morning. He told me there would be a plane traveling past my tree, and that on board were a trio of co-conspirators against our organization."

"He did, did he? And where would he have gotten this information?"

Chevron stumbled at the question. "What—What do you mean?"

"You remember the initiation, surely; it was but two nights ago. Salamandro hadn't even heard of us. What you're suggesting is that, in the span of maybe fourteen hours, he returned to Feuerschloss, got his hands on this piece of information none of the rest of us has seen, and commanded you to action; is that it?"

The verbally-chastised dwarf cast his gaze downward. "I—I guess I didn't think about it. But you remember when I was initiated; I was so excited I looked up every piece of information I could about the Revered! Maybe he did the same, and maybe in doing so—I mean, Feuerschloss is the closest of any of us to the Grecian enclaves, right? Maybe the information came from one of their villages!"

Miranda sighed and brought a hand to her face, massaging her forehead in exasperation. "I suppose this is possible. I'm sorry for yelling at you; this is just going to be a lot of work for me—for all of us, to fix. You should have called a convention to discuss this information at least, before just acting on your own."

"I realize this is going to be rough to fix; just, with the opportunity right there, I couldn't not act! Surely you know how that feels. I couldn't wait to discuss this information; by the time we came to a consensus, they could have been anywhere! They could have been destroying one of our temples, perhaps even killing one of our members!"

Miranda nodded in understanding. "Yes, I see what you were thinking now. We'll still have to discuss this; if the three I saved are indeed plotting to decimate our organization, it would be devastating to the world. We must come up with a plan of action to minimize the threat. Together, though. No more acting on your own about this, understand?"

Chevron nodded solemnly in agreement. "Indeed; we must convene and discuss what to do next. I'm sorry I made you upset."

"Don't worry about it; you did what you thought was the right thing." Miranda embraced the dwarf. "We'll just have to get what information Salamandro has and determine where to go from there."

16

Mission

The jungle that spanned between Flood and Monsoon City provided plentiful shade against the midday sun; the humidity, however, was sweltering for the three northerners, unused to such intense radiative heat. Multiple times, the group had to stop and regain their energy to press onward.

"You know," began Justin as the other three sat on a rock, resting for the umpteenth time, "had I known we were going to be stopping this often, I would have woken everyone up earlier so we might be able to make Monsoon City while it's still light out."

"Sorry Justin, we just aren't accustomed to such incredible heat." Stephen was fanning himself with one of the many short broad leaves that spanned the trail. "You make this trip regularly, and dressed as you are." He motioned to the wizard's long blue robes.

"Yeah; I mean, I think it might get this hot in Chartreuse on the worst summer days, but it's never longer than a few hours." John was hunched over, allowing his excess sweat to drip onto the ground. "You wouldn't happen to know where some water is, would you? I'm parched."

Justin quickly shook his head. "You really don't want to drink the water around here; it causes all sorts of disease."

"More disease than roasting?" Angelo was the next to speak up, re-tying his tunic around his waist; he had opted to go shirtless a few hours before, but the cloth kept getting hung up around his sword, requiring it be re-attached every so often. "I'd at least like to drench myself to cool off; would that be too much to ask?"

Justin shrugged. "I suppose there'd be no harm in that; just don't drink any of it. If you need refreshment, the fruits around here retain enough water that's fit for consumption." Justin looked around, then reached for a large brown bulb. "These are especially good for when you're thirsty; if you crack it open, they contain a sweet juice inside that you can drink right from the husk. It just happens to be mostly water. After that, you can eat the meat on the inside of the husk if you're hungry. That's why they're all along this trail; they proved quite useful to folks in your position." He tossed it to John, who caught it awkwardly; the thing was almost as big as his head.

"Err, that's great and all, but how does one open it?"

"You hit it against something hard, like a rock." Justin made demonstratory hand motions. "Just be careful you don't hurt your fingers doing it. Some people like to crack them open with their foreheads, but I must recommend against this; it tends to hurt a lot more than expected."

John nodded and looked down at the rock he was seated on. He spread his legs a little and bent over, using both hands to grip the fruit and bash it against the stone. After a few swift hits, it split open, an off-white fluid pouring through the crack. The parched man swiftly brought the crack to his lips and began slurping the stuff out, not caring how it tasted.

"Whoa, whoa! Slow down! You're going to make yourself sick, drinking like that!" Justin flailed his arms in a manner the other two found comical. "And watch the spillage; you'll attract insects before too long."

John brought the fruit down from his lips, holding the crack horizontally, then pried the thing in half with his hands. Inside, the fruit was as white as the juice. "Don't worry; I was just really thirsty." He prodded the meat with a finger; it gave a little bit, but was quite firm to the touch. "And you say this part is edible?"

Justin stumbled a bit on his words, not having expected John to stop entirely. "Er, yes, it's similar in flavor to the juice, except stronger. Really, the juice is only water with particulates of the meat of the fruit floating around in it. It's perfectly safe."

Stephen leaned over and sniffed at the fruit in his brother's hands. "Justin, what other fruits are around here? I'm feeling pretty hungry myself, but that—" he pointed to John's fruit "—doesn't really seem . . . appetizing to me. Not that I won't eat it if there's nothing else, but . . ."

"No no, I understand," Justin nodded; "it's an acquired taste for most, really. What kinds of food do you prefer?"

Stephen thought about this for a little bit; it had been a while since he had truly been able to appreciate the flavor of something. "I suppose I enjoy spicy things. John tends to send me the food that doesn't sell in his shop and that he doesn't want to eat himself; I think they're called peppers, the kind I found I enjoy?"

Justin seemed taken aback by this. "You like peppers? I've never liked them myself actually; they don't grow too well in this area due to the shade, but along the trail you might find some if you keep your eyes open. How about you, Angelo was it?"

"As far as fruit goes, I tend to like citrus." The half-elf looked around a bit, plucking a small round thing from a nearby branch. "Like this orange!"

Justin panicked. "Angelo, that's not an orange! It's a—" Angelo screamed and flung the object to the other side of the trail, where it picked itself up and crawled into the foliage. "—spider."

*　　*　　*

Asmodeious' fury had subsided for the time being. Several hours having been wasted lurking, he reasoned with himself that there was only one way anything was going to get done about this nuisance, and that was if he himself did something about it. He was, however, lazy. In the past, he might not have thought twice about destroying Monsoon City just to kill Stephen; nowadays however, these people had developed intricate trade routes and means of travel. If he destroyed that large a center of commerce, Feuerschloss would be swarming with do-gooders trying to "vanquish" him. While it was incredibly unlikely even one of them could lay their sword to his flesh, he didn't feel particularly like putting up with what would surely end up a greater annoyance. Besides, he and his little friend had survived the last town he razed.

No, what he needed was far more absolute, far more certain. His library, however, was proving far too conservative; apparently when mages picked up a pen they decided they needed a shred of morality. Even amongst his more heinous tomes, he could find nothing of any use to him. "You'd think there would be even a ridiculously complex 'Kill That Guy' spell somewhere in here . . ."

Without even thinking, Asmodeious began browsing through his more benign titles in his gardening section. These books had been here when he arrived he recalled; not one seemed useful in the slightest, least of all at the edge of an active volcano, so he had sequestered them in the deepest part of the library, where they had been gathering dust ever since. Absent-mindedly eying over the titles, he was beginning to become crestfallen when something made him double back. "Wait a minute . . ."

He pulled the aged text from the shelf carefully so as not to damage its contents; the pages stuck together in some places due to the ink, but it was nothing irreparable. Leafing through the pages, he finally came across exactly the spell he was looking for. "It'll need a bit of modification I suppose, and maybe . . . yes, but this will do nicely!" He marked the page with a red ribbon and carried the text up to his diabolical magic laboratory, wherein he began furiously scribbling notes in the spellbook's margins as he came up with little modifications and additions. "Diablo! Where are you when I need you? Diablo!"

Asmodeious could hear the half-orc's hurried footsteps bumbling down the stairway. Within a minute, he was in the lab, out of breath. "You . . . (huff) you called . . . (huff) sir?"

The master tossed his gaudy earlier creation at his apprentice, who fumbled with it but eventually gripped it. "You like trinkets, don't you? I need you to stall the vengeance brigade while I prepare something. That there is called an Elemental Summoner; instructions for its use are in my downstairs lab."

"Sir, I'm not allow—"

"I am allowing you access to that lab for this explicit purpose. You are to touch absolutely nothing else, do you understand me?"

Diablo nodded swiftly in understanding, then gasped as he heard something else.

"Salamandro. Come in Salamandro. This is Dryad; can you hear me?"

"Good. Go read up on how to summon; you may practice in the Fencing Room if you like; just be sure you understand what you're doing. I don't want those four knowing anything of what I'm up to." Asmodeious stopped for a second. "Is everything okay, Diablo? You seem a bit fidgety."

Diablo tried desperately to come up with an excuse to leave his master's presence as soon as possible. "Err, well sir, actually . . . I have to use the toilet! And, uhh, you called me down here as I was on my way there! So, if I could please . . ."

"Yes yes, of course, go. Sorry to have kept your bladder waiting." Asmodeious rolled his eyes as his apprentice bolted back up the stairs. "Just don't forget to look at those instructions!"

"Of course not, sir!"

Asmodeious returned to his notes with glee. He knew he would be gathering supplies for some time, but everything would be worth it in the end.

It had been a simple spell meant to control an unwanted ant infestation; with his superior understanding of magic, Asmodeious had re-worked it. With a few amplifications and adjustments, its target and range were far larger. Its crux—and the mage allowed himself a cruel chuckle at this—was the very same relic he had reduced Springsboro to ashes for. With its power, the spell might even wash over the entire sphere of man.

17

Colloquy

The moment Diablo was safely behind the first set of closed doors he could find, he concentrated on responding to Dryad's call. "Dryad? Yes, uh, Salamandro here."

"Salamandro? What took you so long? Couldn't you hear me?"

Diablo struggled to come up with an explanation that did not involve Asmodeious in some way. "Well, uhh, you see, I mean, yes, I heard you, but . . . I didn't know how to respond! You know how it is, first days on new legs and all that, heh . . ." He tried to not let his nervousness show. "Anyway, I figured it out now. What's up?"

Dryad knew there was something wrong with the way Salamandro had responded, but said nothing about it. "We've all been summoned for discussion and deliberation regarding a new—" He paused. "Anyway, we're all meeting in the Roaming Edifice—oh, that's where you were inducted; I forgot you didn't know its name—so, because you haven't set up your meditation chamber yet, we need you to be somewhere we can pick you up."

Diablo sighed with mild relief; It seemed as though his excuse had been bought. But what was this summoning about? "Very well; I'll be . . ." He knew he couldn't go out the front door without Asmodeious hearing, and he'd really be in trouble if he couldn't explain himself for that. "I'll be on the roof of Feuerschloss again; that worked last time, right?"

"Yes, that will be acceptable; we shall be there within ten minutes. Be prepared."

Diablo nodded to no one in particular and made his way to the third floor lab as swiftly and silently as possible. Indeed, he could see the telltale bank of clouds approaching, from the north this time. Not wanting to be caught off-guard again, he closed his eyes and waited.

And waited.

"Salamandro?"

Diablo leaped backwards in surprise, almost sliding to the edge of the platform at the sudden interruption of his waiting by Chevron's voice. Looking up, he found the dwarf was indeed right in front of him, alongside Rhox. "Is everything okay?"

"Oh, uhh, yeah; you just startled me, is all." Diablo stood and brushed himself off out of habit. "So what's all this about?"

Chevron and Rhox exchanged glances. "You'll find out," responded the larger half-orc; "don't worry, it's nothing too major, I don't think. Come; everyone else has convened in the throne room."

The three peers passed through the cloud-lined hallway to the central room Diablo recognized from earlier as the place he had first met the group. Indeed, this was only his second time actually seeing any of them, and their collective bearing still made him nervous.

Unlike the previous time Diablo had been there, all the thrones were organized in a large heptagon with one point missing. As Chevron and Rhox returned to their respective seats, Diablo moved towards the empty vertex, knowing it had been meant for him. With the entire assembly gathered, Miranda rose to speak.

"Thank you all for coming; I realize that for many of us this is a bit of an inconvenience, but after some discussion, Chevron and I both decided this was necessary. Chevron, if you would please."

Miranda returned to her throne as Chevron rose again. "Yes; yesterday morning, I purposefully induced a microburst in the vicinity of Monsoon City, in the upper troposphere." Dryad and Manas both became visibly upset at this revelation. "Now now, let me finish. I realize this is going to be a lot of work to restore; as Miranda stated before, we already discussed the repercussions of my actions and I take full responsibility."

"That's easy to say," began Dryad.

"I know you're upset by this development, and that's enough at this point. We can discuss what needs to be done about that at a later date. Presently however, there are more pressing issues. I started this atmospheric disturbance on a tip from one of our very own; a plane was traveling in this vicinity, and I was informed that on-board were individuals involved in a plot to bring about an end to the Revered."

Everyone but Miranda stood, all trying to get a word in regarding this new development. "Everyone, please!" Luna's voice rang out over the tumult, and all fell silent again. "Let Chevron finish; I'm sure all our questions and concerns are the same, and I'm sure we'll find everything out soon enough."

"Thank you, Luna." The half-elf nodded and resumed her seat. "Now, the plane did crash; however, Miranda was not privy to the same information I was and saved three of the plane's passengers. She was, unfortunately or not, unable to save the pilot in time. As such, we may very well still have a threat on our hands. I believe the only individual amongst us who will be able to answer whether or not this is true is the one who informed me of the threat in the first place—Salamandro, if you would."

Diablo took a nervous gulp and stepped forward. *This was all my fault! But I may still be able to turn this to my advantage.* He took a deep breath, composed himself, and began. "Indeed, my information seems quite accurate, as even now the survivors have met up with a fourth collaborator and approach Monsoon City."

"Salamandro, how did you come across this information?" Miranda asked, genuinely curious. She knew Chevron's guess, but wanted to know what the new half-orc had heard.

Diablo stumbled a little, but not enough to lose face. "I—well, Feuerschloss is in the Mountains, and there are some Grecian villages in relative proximity where I am known. I was curious about this new group into which I was inducted, and in asking around this piece of information crossed my ears. Admittedly acting on impulse, I requested Chevron's assistance, knowing of his location and influence."

Everyone in the circle nodded; Dryad was the first to speak up. "You seem to be keeping rather close tabs on this group; have you determined exactly what their plot is?"

Diablo shrugged. "I suppose they'll just try to off each of us, one by one. It's not like I can read their minds."

Dryad nodded, apparently appeased by this response. "As we cannot ascertain these dubious allegations, I do not believe such mortal actions should be taken just yet."

"I agree," responded Rhox; "as disastrous as it might be to lose even one of our members, to kill even one innocent would strip us of the right to call ourselves the Revered. Not that I'm condemning your actions, Chevron." The dwarf nodded in understanding.

"So then," began Miranda, "what shall we do about this?"

Dryad was again the one to speak up. "I believe a tribunal to be in order. Give me a day to prepare—Luna, if I may request your assistance as well—I believe I can come up with exactly what is needed."

"I shall assist, if it will determine the innocence or guilt of this party." Luna nodded to Dryad in agreement with his terms. "Is everyone in concurrence with this decision?"

One by one, the members of the assembly nodded.

"Very well," replied Miranda; "Let us adjourn for now, to meet back here in three days with a decision from Dryad and Luna. Thank you for your help in this matter, Salamandro."

Diablo blushed at the praise. "Don't mention it! Just doing my duty."

With that, each member stood and moved to leave the chamber. Worried about possibly being scolded by his master again upon returning in the same manner he had last time, Diablo ran to Chevron. "Err, Chevron, is there a way I could go without, you know, meteorizing? Like how I get here?"

"Why do you ask?"

"Well, last time I did it, the volcano didn't take too well to it; Feuerschloss is rather precariously perched, you know?"

Chevron nodded. "Yes, I suppose that could be a problem. The one you need to talk to is Luna; she should be able to transport you back to the ground, probably in the area of your castle. Besides, you'll need to talk to her eventually anyway about setting up your meditation chamber."

"Meditation chamber?" Diablo looked at both halls he hadn't accessed yet. "Is that where—"

"Oh, my apologies; I suppose we never did discuss it with you. Every member of the Revered is allowed a room in this, the Roaming Edifice, in which to meditate; for the rest of us, it is also the means by which we get here. You'll want to set up a link to it from somewhere within your castle."

Diablo nodded; "It would be rather nice to not have to wait for this thing to come to Feuerschloss every time I need to be here."

"Well, be quick; Luna will want to discuss Dryad's plans, so you should catch her as soon as possible."

Diablo again nodded, then ran across the gathering chamber to where the half-elf and halfling were just beginning to leave. "Luna! Do you have a moment?"

Luna signaled to Dryad to go ahead of her. "Of course Salamandro; anything for a fellow Revered. How can I be of assistance?"

"Chevron says you're the person to talk to about transportation, and a meditation chamber?"

"Oh yes; Rhox should have at least begun construction on your platform at this point. Let's go set up your transportation link. I believe it was decided before that you'd be positioned in the opposite hall; shall we?" The half-elf confidently led the way.

As they turned left and progressed down this new hall, Diablo admired the sandstone handiwork of the wall. "This place really is solid, isn't it?"

"Rhox wouldn't be a Revered if he did shoddy construction. Ah, there it is, ahead."

Sure enough, there seemed to be a point where the hallway had been extended much more recently, and to the right was a short path out into the sky leading to a relatively small square platform. "Eventually," explained Luna, "this will become your meditation chamber; you'll have to talk to Rhox about what kind of internal construction you desire. If you wish, you may examine other rooms for inspiration. For now however, we'll just set up the transportation link."

The half-elf stepped down the precarious path, stopping just short of the platform. She uttered a few words Diablo couldn't make out, and before her appeared what seemed to be two coins. Taking both, she tossed one into the very center of the square; she then turned and handed Diablo the other. "When you return to your castle, place this in a hidden location on the floor. It shall allow you to transport up here whenever you wish. Now, for the matter of getting you back down there in the first place . . ."

"Err, could you try to—" Diablo stopped himself. Indeed, it would be far easier for him to appear on the roof again, but to request it might seem suspicious.

"Try to . . . what?"

"Oh, um, just try to get me as close to the castle as you can." The half-orc allowed himself another nervous chuckle.

"Of course. Now close your eyes and concentrate on the castle."

Diablo did as he was told; he heard the half-elf utter a few words, then for a brief moment felt her hand upon his forehead. When he opened his eyes, he was once again in the open-air laboratory.

18

Skepticism

Monsoon City was visible long before the group reached it; brilliant lights atop the increasingly-traveled path led the four through the otherwise non-traversable nighttime jungle. As Justin had predicted, sunset had occurred over two hours before, meaning by this point the only illumination they had was that of the city. At least without the light of the sun bearing down on them, the jungle had become much more bearable.

"Has the swelling gone down, Angelo?" Stephen was genuinely concerned for the well-being of his friend; the spider from earlier had managed to bite him before he flung it across the trail.

"Stephen, I wouldn't worry too much about it," Justin reassured the man for what had to have been the twelfth time; "the venom is mildly painful, but even without treatment it's not debilitating."

Angelo could feel his hand throbbing from the bite; however, as Justin's many reassurances had stated, it never moved any further than his lower arm. Of course, he couldn't see if the swelling had gone down in the dark, so he remained silent, tenderly massaging the wound.

As they finally stepped out of the shade of the jungle, John whistled in admiration at the sight before them. "I'd heard tales about it, but never had the chance to see it myself. This is Monsoon City's gaming strip, isn't it?"

Before them, the path opened into a wide street, both sides flanked by neon, steel, and glass. Overwhelming at first glance, details in the varying structures were visible as they were concentrated upon. The buildings all seemed to run together, rising out of the ground like the cliffs to the east.

The noise was almost deafening, sounds of numerous people and machines all occupying such a small space trying to drown each other out.

Justin nodded. "Gambling is perhaps the biggest source of income for the city; it's a wonderfully ingenious concept, really. Everything's indoors, so there's no need to close it down during the monsoon season. Because it's dangerous to venture outside when it's raining like that, the only thing for patrons to do is gamble some more. Of course, that's the lull of their business, as no new customers dare make the journey here in such conditions."

Stephen was busy watching something he could barely make out over the skyline, what appeared to be a moving light display on the Cliffs of Chevron. "What's going on over there?"

"Oh, that's the light show," explained Justin. "They do something new every week, or at least try to; as long as they've been doing that, I'm sure they've done a few repeats. Besides, I know some of their more popular shows have been displayed more than once. Anyway, I realize this is everyone's first visit, but we aren't here for sightseeing, remember? We're going to have to get to sleep as early as possible tonight; tomorrow's going to be a long day, regardless of what we choose to do." The wizard began leading the way towards the west, where his lab lay.

"What do you mean, what we choose to do?" Angelo asked. "Aren't we trying to stop whatever it was that destroyed Springsboro?"

"Certainly, that is the eventual goal; however, shouldn't we try to find out as much about our adversary beforehand as we can? I figure our choices are head east tomorrow for Feuerschloss, or head west for River City and perhaps some clarity behind all this."

Stephen shook his head. "We've spent enough time dawdling; it's time for action."

John shrugged; either direction was detrimental in his opinion. "Whatever you guys want to do; I'm too tired to worry about it right now."

"I agree with Stephen; we spent all of today just getting here," Angelo pointed out. "How long would you estimate it might take us to get to Feuerschloss if we started tomorrow anyway?"

Justin contemplated the distance. "Under normal circumstances, it would be three days at a grueling pace; however, considering what we just accomplished, it's looking more like five."

"A difference of two days? What's your definition of 'grueling'?"

"Six hours of sleep a night. Such would be devastating to our physical and mental health however, so I must strongly recommend against moving that swiftly. We shall require all faculties operating in top shape if we are to face our adversary and have any chance of succeeding, I fear."

"You see?" Stephen ran ahead of the group, stopping everyone. "Five days? That's more than enough time for us to meet an untimely death; we were already almost killed in that plane crash. Do we really need to take this proposed detour?"

"Stephen, we have no idea what we're up against. For all we know, the Revered want you dead; that's a big deal. River City's ruins might hold answers! We can't just ignore that fact and charge blindly at Feuerschloss."

"Nor can we just ignore the timeline we have, Justin. None of us has ever been to these ruins besides you; we're likely to get lost. You're the only one who might know what to look for, if there's anything actually there worth looking for. It would be a massive waste of time. I remember seeing the site marked on your map; it would take us at least a day to get there, not to mention exploration and getting back. That's three additional days that could be used in getting us closer to what we already know our eventual goal is anyway."

"But Stephen, how are we going to progress once we get there?"

"We already know the Revered of Fire is the one we'll find at Feuerschloss; that narrows down our plan of attack pretty well, I'd think."

"Guys, guys!" John stepped between the two. "I know this is important, but it won't mean anything if we don't get some sleep first. I know I'm not the only one of us who's exhausted after a day of hiking through that sweltering overgrowth. Justin, if you'd be so kind?"

Justin sighed and shrugged. "Whatever. Tomorrow I guess we'll head towards Feuerschloss; maybe at some point on the way there we'll figure out what exactly it is we're supposed to be doing." He stepped past the now dumbfounded John, leading the way once again.

"That's not exactly what I meant, but hey, it got us somewhere." Angelo found himself agreeing with the man for once; indeed, everyone needed rest.

Justin led the other three down several back alleys and side streets, all the while not speaking. Finally, he stopped in front of a short, small, unassuming brick building. "This is the place." He pulled a rather large keyring out of his robes and began fiddling with it. "Now which one was it . . ."

"Justin. I was beginning to suspect you weren't going to be in this evening." The elf almost dropped his keys as the source of the new voice stepped out of the shadows beside the domicile. An immense, bulging silhouette sporting a well-made hat, the man straightened his lapels and stepped between the group and the door.

"Oh! Heh, hi there, Mickey . . ." Justin stuttered. "I uh, I didn't expect you here!"

The man smiled and nodded, removing his headgear and revealing a completely bald scalp. "Very few expect me when I've arrived," he retorted with a thick accent, "though really they should. Surely you know why I am paying you this house call."

Justin tried to crack a nervous smile, but it came out entirely wrong. "D—Don't call me Sh—Shirl—"

"I'll call a delinquent whatever I want to, bub." Mickey gripped the much smaller elf by his robes, spun him around and slammed him against the door. "You're late on rent this month. You know how Don feels about that."

Justin swallowed, not daring to squirm. "L—Late? Is it past due already? Oh dear me, I must have lost track of the ti—"

"You know rent is due on the first, Justin. Don't lie. Now, where's that money?"

Justin closed his eyes, quaking in fear. "I—I don't have it right now."

Mickey shook his head. "Justin, you disappoint me. When has Don ever done wrong to you? He doesn't raise your rent; he hasn't demanded tributes or sacrifices, and yet this is the second time you've been late."

Justin looked over his assailant's shoulder. "Mickey, I appreciate the visit and all, but can we—can we discuss this some other time? I have guests."

The mountainous man set the mage down and turned. "Ah yes, my sincerest apologies; my name's Mickey. I work under Don Kane, the man who owns this property." Upon seeing their visibly shaken expressions he returned his hat to his head and gave a curt nod. "Don't you worry; my present business involves none of you." He turned back to look again at Justin. "Three days. Don wants his money, or your shit's going on the street. Good luck finding another place in this town when that happens."

Justin nodded and waved nervously in understanding. "Three days, got it. I'll do what I can."

Mickey let out a gruff and left the scene, lumbering down the road they had approached on. As soon as he was no longer visible, Justin heaved a sigh of relief. "Glad that's over." He returned his attention to his overloaded key ring.

After an awkward pause, Stephen stepped up to the fumbling wizard. "Justin, I'm sorry about ear—"

"Not right now, Stephen; I have to figure out which key goes to this—" He pulled one out and tried it. "—door. Damn. Besides, you were right."

Stephen was taken back by this comment. "I was? I mean, I know what I argued was what I wanted to do, but—"

"You were. Damn!" Another key failed. "I still believe a bit more preparation is important, but perhaps it isn't necessary. As you said—Damn! As you said, the one we'll find at Feuerschloss will undoubtedly be the Revered of Fire. I guess I was more concerned with what might happen between now and then, but honestly there's nothing that can prepare us for that more than getting—Ah!" The lock clicked and turned, allowing the door to open. "—getting the rest we all already need. After you."

*   *   *

Luna stepped from her portal into Dryad's throne room. Situated deep within the Tree of Life, the chamber was surprisingly large, but not so much in floor space as in head room; high above, the trunk opened up to the sky, nothing but a canopy of leaves and the plant's immense size protecting the interior from the elements. The room had not been carved out of the living wood; rather, the tree had been coerced to grow around it, creating the enclosure naturally; Luna already knew this, but it was made obvious by the bark covering the walls and floor as well. Almost perfectly round, the chamber branched off to the half-elf's left, directly across from the throne itself; she knew this path led deeper into the trunk of the tree, into a labyrinth designed to make this place inaccessible to all but those who knew the way.

Dryad was sitting upon his throne, clearly deep in thought after the meeting. Luna could understand why; as Miranda had pointed out, Chevron's actions would mean quite a bit of work for the diminutive Revered. "Contemplating where to begin in assisting rebuilding Monsoon City's crops next year?"

The halfling looked up in surprise. "Oh, Luna; I hadn't noticed you come in." He sighed, resting his chin in his palm. "It's not that; while that is certainly vexing, I find myself pondering our newest member's actions far more."

"Salamandro? What has he done?"

Dryad looked up at Luna, a look of concern on his face. "Luna, I requested your assistance in probing this suspected group of conspirators in the hopes that I might confide in you. Of all our fellows, your philosophical leanings would be most likely to take what I fear with the necessary grain of salt, if you will, while still taking it seriously enough to help me. Can I trust you in this?"

Luna seemed a little taken aback by this sudden change of character in her friend. "Whatever this is, it has clearly upset you; I swear, I shall do as you request. Now, what's going on?"

Dryad laid his head in his hands and began. "When I contacted Salamandro yesterday through our mind-link, it took him quite some time to respond. His reasoning for this was that he was still new to all this stuff, so he hadn't quite figured out *how* to respond." Luna nodded in understanding; indeed, the half-orc had been ordained just a few days before, and it wasn't as though anything pressing had happened since. "But, that's just the thing—how had he contacted Chevron?"

Luna paused. "What do you mean?"

"I mean, it was his tip that encouraged Chevron to produce that microburst, right? He was the one who had heard the rumor circulating about a group trying to destroy our order; how had he communicated this to Chevron, if not through our mind-link?"

"I see where you're going with this; indeed, he had no knowledge of the meditation chambers, and certainly hadn't a transportation link to the Edifice until I made one for him after the meeting. He had to have used the mind-link."

"Yes, but if that's the case, why did he lie?" Dryad scratched the back of his head. "It makes no sense. Something about his story isn't adding up, and I don't know what part is true and what part is false." He looked up into his friend's eyes. "I can't trust him, which is a serious problem; he's one of us now! One of my peers! I must trust him if we are to work together as a unit. But this blatant lie . . . What should I make of it?"

Luna nodded, sitting on the armrest beside the halfling. "I see now why you were so shaken. He took time to respond, but did so eventually; that was the nature of the lie, was it not?"

Dryad nodded. "He stated he hadn't figured out the nature of the mind-link yet, so he couldn't respond immediately. But that clearly cannot be the case!"

"Calm down," Luna spoke, resting her hand upon her friend's shoulder, trying to comfort him; "if what I understand from you and what I have experienced of Salamandro are all true, then my assumption based on the circumstances is that he is trying to hide something. It's very likely he is trying to hide it from the Revered as a whole, not just you."

Dryad nodded; "That is the same conclusion I came to. But what do we do about this? We can't just barge in and demand he share this with us; I mean, he's entitled to a private life the same as the rest of us! What if it's just something he's ashamed of?"

"Let us just follow the wishes of the Revered for now," Luna proposed; "if we assume this is a harmless misspeaking on his part, I'm sure Salamandro will be grateful for our not prying. Besides, a possible threat on our order is the more important priority right now, is it not?"

Dryad sighed and nodded. "I suppose you're right. If it turns out to be problematic in the future, we can always bring it up privately with him if need be. And yes, we have more important things to worry about right now."

Luna smiled down at her friend. "Are we settled then?"

The halfling grinned and nodded. "I think so."

"Am I to assume then that you haven't prepared anything for our Inquisition?"

"Of course not; I've been too concerned with this . . . no matter. What do you believe would be the best course of action for confronting these four young men?"

And so the two spent the entire night discussing the upcoming Inquisition—what to ask, how to ask it, how to approach the group, everything had to be exactly perfect if they were to determine the truth of such a strong accusation.

*   *   *

Justin's laboratory was surprisingly stocked for what Stephen quite rightfully pointed out was basically a bachelor pad. Indeed, the "lab" really only consisted of one room in the small building, set aside from what had obviously been refashioned into living quarters for the elf. Plenty of non-perishable food filled the cupboards, and though there was only one bed, Justin had an entire chest of blankets and sheets the other three could use to sleep in for the following nights. Being that he made regular trips out to the ruins of River City, a destination of a day's travel away, the wizard even had a tent big enough for the entire group should conditions prove unsavory enough to warrant its use (and Justin assured them multiple times, conditions in the forests to come most definitely would prove such). So, with everything they thought they could possibly need for their coming trip set aside and prepared for the morning, the four took to sleep; they all knew the journey forth would be rough, and they would need all the rest they could muster.

19

Inquisition

The first rays of morning light filtered through the window of Justin's bedroom, casting a checkered pattern on the carpet as a result of the blinds and the bars over the glass. The warmth of sunlight worked its magic on Stephen, Angelo, and John, waking them pleasantly from their slumber; it was the first time in days they had awoken to greet the sun, and it put all three of them in a good mood to start their day. Justin slept a little longer, but then he was the one who got the proper mattress; such could only be expected of the admittedly lazy wizard. They let him sleep in for about a half-hour, during which they all prepared their weapons and armor for the day's trek. Stephen felt it was probably a good idea to go ahead and wake him up after this; they did need to get on the road soon, after all.

"Justin. Justin?" He prodded the slumbering elf with the stick end of a broom he'd found in a closet. "Come on; we have to get going."

The mage mumbled, rolling over. "Five minutes . . ."

Stephen rolled his eyes. "We've given you half an hour now. Seriously, we need to get moving now if we want to make some tracks. Remember, Feuerschloss? Three days at a grueling pace, more likely five?" He unceremoniously ripped the blankets off the bed. "I'm not playing around; let's go!"

Justin sighed and rolled back over towards his assailant. "If you insist."

"You know I do." He threw the sheets back at the elf. "Now get ready; everyone else is itching to get on the road."

Stephen left Justin alone in his room to prepare. It didn't take him very long; he had slept in the robes he intended to travel in, and everything he had been designated to carry had already been packed save for the blankets he'd slept on. With minimal fuss and little worry from anyone else, the group departed the building toward the rising sun.

"The city seems a lot quieter now as opposed to last night," Angelo observed. "I know it's still early, but surely there are businesses open at this hour?"

Justin nodded and re-adjusted his load on his back; everything had been tied up in his sheets, making for a rather cumbersome pack. "There are; however, most of what we saw last night was the gaming district, as John pointed out. The strip tends to go quiet after sunrise; a lot of the gamblers take the opportunity to get some sleep. Those who don't have usually passed out in their own rooms anyway from drinking too heavily."

"Drinking?"

"You know, alcohol. Booze. Spirits and the like. People come here to relax and let loose; for many, that's how they like to."

Angelo shrugged; "I suppose I'll never understand that sentiment."

Stephen patted his friend on the shoulder and smirked. "Don't worry; I'm sure it will make more sense when you grow up."

"Hey! I'm plenty grown up, thank you very much!"

"And that's exactly what I said when I started going through puberty."

Angelo started chasing Stephen in mock anger; the human just ran ahead, laughing. Justin watched the two cavort and shrugged.

"As I said, people like to come here to relax; I see they're already getting into the spirit of the place."

John chuckled. "Stephen always was one to joke around; I'm glad he's found a friend he can relate with like this."

Much of their walk through Monsoon City proceeded in this manner; Stephen and Angelo eventually ran out of energy in the outskirts of town however, and the four decided they would stop for a short breakfast pick-up once they reached the Cliffs of Chevron.

"So, how did these cliffs form?" Stephen asked as he bit into a piece of jerky. Justin peered up at the rock face and shrugged.

"You know, I actually don't know. I know the sheer rises are the result of the winds higher up; they hit the point almost directly and split against the cliffs. As for how they originally formed though, I really haven't the slightest idea."

John bit into a fruit he picked in the jungle the day before, also looking up at the wall before them. "Could it have been artificially constructed?"

Justin looked at the man, confused by the notion. "What do you mean?"

"Well, I mean, what if people had made it? Is it possible?"

Justin shook his head. "Incredibly unlikely. The Tree of Wind is clearly rooted at the top, and the Enchanted Rainforest surrounds that for some distance."

"The Enchanted Rainforest?" Angelo entered the conversation, setting his food aside for the moment. "I've never heard of this place."

"It's not surprising; you didn't know who the Revered were, so it's doubtful you'd have heard of their garden." Justin pulled his map out and spread it on a nearby rock. "This area here, from the Cliffs over to the Mountains, is encompassed by the Enchanted Rainforest. It is a place entirely tended to by the Revered; within its bounds are three of these special locations marked by runes." He pointed them out as he named them. "The Tree of Wind, the Lake on the Pillar, and the Lunar Pyramid. Each of these places is spoken of in legends, but it is doubtful any man has ever gotten close enough to truly observe them, besides those of the Revered. It could be that this Rainforest was set up specifically to protect the group, at least originally."

Stephen nodded, digesting this information even as he did the same with his breakfast. "So it's likely that, if the Revered have something to do with why Springsboro was burned down, we'll have to venture through this forest."

Justin looked at the map, clearly not looking forward to such a prospect. "I suppose so; let's set that thought aside for now, though. Remember, our first clues won't be conclusive until we get to Feuerschloss."

They finished their short breakfast in silence, then proceeded along the southern cliff face; they found it easier to stay as close to the massive formation as possible, as the rock provided a sort of natural trail through the forest.

"Say, Justin," began Stephen a few hours after they had been moving, "the foliage here is different from the stuff we traveled through yesterday; it's also not quite as stuffy. Doesn't this place get as much rain as the city?"

Justin hefted his pack and moved up to Stephen's side. "Yes, it does; recall, the wind breaks almost perfectly evenly against the cliff point. However, on this side of the cliffs, the water washes most of the topsoil south; the lush jungle can't survive in what remains. The result is this coniferous forest; these trees are far more accustomed to clinging to what little soil they can find."

Stephen nodded. "I suppose that makes sense."

And suddenly everything went black.

*   *   *

Stephen wasn't sure when or even if he had come to; everything around him was darkness. When he brought his hand to his face however, he could see it; he could be dreaming he realized, but at least he was conscious.

"My greetings." He looked before him, to where the voice had originated; a figure faded into existence, short in stature. Completely bald, the being seemed to be draped in brown silks, a pair of matching leggings covering his lower half. A cape that seemed fashioned of ivy leaves sprouted from his shoulders, trailing along the ground behind him.

"Who are you!?" Angelo stood and defiantly drew his sword.

"You unsheathe your weapon before you know who you intend to use it against?" The being raised his eyebrow. "You are lucky to be alive still with that attitude."

John shakily rose to his feet, looking around the darkness for anything else. "Where are my companions?"

"That is not important right now; I assure you they are safe, however."

Justin was barely paying the man any attention, instead far more interested in what was going on around him. "Oh, wow! Such a wonderfully-crafted illusion . . . this is an Inquisition from the Revered, isn't it? I've never had the chance to see Luna's work in person . . . And you must be Dryad! Am I right? Wow; I never imagined I'd live to see a member of the Revered like this!"

"Calm yourself!" Dryad crossed his arms and closed his eyes, trying to be as patient as he could with the over-excited elf. "This is an Inquisition; however, it is you who shall be answering my questions, not the other way around."

Stephen shrugged off the initial shock of his situation. "Questions? You already know of our existence, so you must know much about us; what more could you possibly hope to glean?"

The halfling smirked. "Clearly you have an understanding of the situation you are in. In truth, I was asked to prepare whatever questions I felt would be necessary in determining your . . . guilt."

"Guilt!?" Angelo pointed his sword at the diminutive man. "What guilt could we possibly carry?"

"Put that thing away before I take it away." Dryad did not lose an ounce of his poise as he stared the half-elf down, a truly stunning feat for one so comparatively short. "You may, in fact, have no guilt; that is why I am here. Were there no question, the Inquisition would not take place."

John crossed his arms defiantly at the little man. "And what, pray tell, are these questions you simply must ask me?"

"You see, I was asked to prepare the necessary questions; however, in the end, I found I only really had one question I wanted to ask."

Justin nodded. "Of course; the Revered would have no need to ask but one question. With what, then, must you inquire?"

Dryad took a deep breath, preparing himself. "Why do you continue your trek to Feuerschloss?"

Stephen paused and pondered the question carefully. He knew this journey might bring the group in direct opposition of the Revered if it proved necessary, something most anyone in the world would probably find reprehensible if they knew who or what the Revered were. As such, he knew he had to answer carefully. "I continue because I feel I must help several thousand rest in peace."

Angelo's answer was far more immediate. "Clearly you know enough of our quest to have found us; surely then you must have noticed? Something . . . wrong is going on. I—no, we intend to find out what."

John contemplated as Stephen had; however, his ulterior motives made him more wary. He did not want to reveal too much to this stranger; things might get leaked to the wrong people. "I suppose you could say the purpose of my quest is to destroy that which destroys."

Justin clearly knew who this questioner was—were the Revered actually concerned about this quest? This could lead credence to the hypothesis that they were involved with the Springsboro incident. "I travel with my companions to get to the bottom of things, and to finally understand just what is going on around here."

Dryad smiled. "Thank you for your cooperation; it is most appreciated." And all four passed out once again. The lights came up within the interrogation chamber, and the halfling turned to his companion. "What do you think?"

Luna looked deep in thought, glancing over the still forms of the four. "I'm not sure. They all knew of Feuerschloss without any further explanation, so that's definitely their destination; however I don't believe they intend to pose a threat to the Revered as a whole."

"Yes, that's what I thought as well. Their answers . . . they almost seem to lend support to my earlier concerns about Salamandro's actions. Maybe they intend to uncover something we ourselves have overlooked."

Luna shook her head. "This is distressing; I do not wish to think of a peer in such a way."

"Aye, I understand. What then shall we do about these four?"

Luna contemplated, then turned to the halfling. "I say we let them finish their quest."

"Are you sure? I mean, they may very well end up killing our latest inductee, or at least trying."

The half-elf nodded. "Indeed, one of them did state that he intended to destroy that which destroys; one could see fire very easily as a destructive force. However, I think the words of the younger human ring with more noble purpose. To help thousands rest in peace? What do you suppose he could mean?"

Dryad shrugged. "You can't ignore the possibility that he could have meant the destruction of the world with such language."

"True; however, I believe he would not have used those words were that the case. No, I wonder if he refers to an event that has already occurred, outside our scope."

"That seems incredibly unlikely."

"Indeed, but it is possible. Truly, Salamandro has his secrets; what if something happened to these four that someone is trying to hide?"

Dryad nodded. "So you're proposing we let them go to Feuerschloss without impeding, but keep an eye on them?"

"That is exactly what I'm proposing. And furthermore, I wonder if we should speed their progress, to better determine what to bring to the counsel in two days."

"I suppose that makes sense. What then shall we do with them?"

Luna waved her hand in front of herself, and a map of the world appeared before the pair. She pointed to their location at the Lunar Pyramid. "We've got them here right now, and it's about noon. Let's drop them right here, just south of the edge of the Rainforest? That way, they still have the option of turning back if they decide not to continue, but are far closer to their goal. In addition, this would provide us a particularly good vantage point to continue observing them."

Dryad nodded, looking over the map. "They could probably get to Feuerschloss by tomorrow morning from there as well. I agree with your decision." He looked back down at the four. "Do you want to do the honors?"

Luna stepped forward through the map, up to where the four lay unconscious on her palace floor. She recited a short incantation, and they were transported to the point on the map. "Their location should appear there; this way, we can keep proper tabs on them from here."

"I hope you're right about this."

"So do I."

20

Hindrance

Diablo had immediately darted down to Asmodeious' lower laboratory to obtain the text he had referred to before the half-orc's sudden summoning, following his return. He knew his master would be livid with him if he didn't start working on mastering this new device as soon as possible. He took the text back up to the practice chamber as he had been instructed and began reading over the pages that detailed the Summoner's use. Of course, he realized quite soon thereafter that he really didn't have much in the way of substance in the room to practice with outside of air. The apprentice shrugged and turned to the appropriate page, then thrust his arm forth towards the mostly empty room. "Air!"

For a second, Diablo wasn't sure anything had happened; however, the wind whistled around a point before the mage, and before long a small air distortion appeared before him in the shape of a mannequin. The figure wandered around in a circle as Diablo again referenced the tome, looking at the various commands he could give the new elemental. He decided to start simple; besides, he reasoned, he'd have to work with the commands for all elementals most likely anyway.

"Walk forward." The elemental reacted as expected, walking in a straight line in front of itself. "Stop." It did so. "Turn twenty degrees left. Back-flip." The tiny biped did as commanded every time, quite responsive in its actions. Diablo continued with these simple commands, getting used to the response time of the elemental before going on into the more specific commands.

"Chill." The figure jumped, then seemed to disappear; Diablo wasn't sure what was going on until he suddenly felt a very cold breeze whip through his clothing, chilling him thoroughly. The half-orc shivered, having not expected such immediate results; "Stop." The elemental reappeared before him. "Let's see . . . lift." Diablo indicated the book; the elemental walked forward and picked it up effortlessly. "Up." It jumped and levitated, still holding the book. "Okay, down. Put it down."

Diablo understood now the utility of such summons; however, he also knew that these simple things were not the sorts of things he'd need them to do. He pulled a small training totem from against a wall to the center of the room. After catching his breath, he pointed to it: "Attack."

The figure immediately leaped into action once again, charging at the totem. It struck at the wooden structure with its limbs in a seemingly random manner, something Diablo knew would never be very useful against anything or anyone. He looked again to the text for guidance. "It says I can influence attack patterns if I concentrate. Let's see . . ." He focused on his hand-to-hand training he received from Asmodeious; sure enough, the elemental began following a set pattern, focusing its motions on both blocking and striking in good positions. *Yes, this will work!* thought Diablo with a grin. *I just might be able to hold them off with this. At the very least, they'll have some difficulty reaching the castle, which is all Asmodeious said he needed.* The half-orc, done with his training, dissolved the elemental and ran upstairs to his own laboratory to see where exactly the group had gotten to.

What he saw with his cauldron made him worry. He ran upstairs to the open-air lab to verify the time; indeed, the sun was only just past overhead. "It's hardly afternoon. I couldn't have been down there for more than a day; that's absurd. How on earth . . ." He ran back down to his cauldron. Sure enough, the four were almost into the Mountains already.

"Asmodeious is going to have my head if I don't start right now . . . how they got this far is beyond me, but they'll have to get through my elementals if they want to make it any further." Diablo wasn't sure his plan would work, but he was certainly going to try. He thrust his arm at the scene in his cauldron. "Rock."

* * *

"So, did you guys experience that too?" Stephen scratched his head as he sat up, peering at his new surroundings.

Angelo nodded and felt for his sword; sure enough, it had been re-sheathed. "I suppose we all did. The Inquisition, you mean?"

"Yeah. Err, also, where are we?"

The scenery was very different from what any of them recalled seeing when they had blacked out. A cliff face was still present to their immediate north, though it was far shorter than the Cliffs of Chevron; these looked relatively easy to scale as well, at least from their vantage point. The Mountains loomed over them, far more immediate than they ever seemed before. Justin scratched his head, then pulled his map back out.

"I believe we had been here when we were called to the Inquisition," he stated, pointing at a location along the familiar Cliffs of Chevron. "Based on the height of the Mountains . . . I think we might be right here." He pointed to a spot just south of what he had earlier designated the Lunar Pyramid. "This would also make sense if my hypothesis is correct, that the Inquisition chamber was provided by Luna herself. She dropped us off right outside her own palace."

"But why would she do that?" John seemed both worried and puzzled. "Wouldn't she want us to not go any further?"

"Ah, but the Inquisitor was not Luna, but Dryad. He's a very different individual. It's entirely possible the two of them conversed about our fate; indeed, we were not in there for an hour, but look at the position of the sun." It had easily been an hour by the looks of it; the sun was now just past overhead. "We were probably unconscious for their decision."

"That doesn't seem very fair," stated Angelo. "Shouldn't we get a say in their decision?"

"We did; that was the Inquisition. Clearly, they chose to put us closer to our goal, but not at it. Perhaps they intend to watch and see what exactly we do."

Stephen nodded. "I guess that makes sense. Here's hoping they don't decide to kill us for pressing onward."

Justin clambered to his feet and rushed ahead of the impatient human. "Stephen, how could you think that? The Revered just directly addressed us regarding our quest! This is a big deal; they already know where we intend to go, and they might know what it is we might have to do. We can't risk this!"

"And that's exactly why we must risk it!" Stephen stood, facing the elf directly. "We're turning heads; this is a good sign. I take this to mean we're on the right track. We'll figure out what's going on if we press further! We can't be but a day from the castle at this point! They want us to go!"

"What if this is a test? What if they want us to turn back?"

"Guys, I hate to interrupt your argument," interjected John, "but Justin, might you know what that thing is?" He pointed to the ground a few feet in front of the pair, where a small figure had sprung from the earth. The elf turned to observe this new being.

"I—I don't know. I've never seen anything like it." Justin knelt down to get a better look at it. The figure was very simplistic in shape, but clearly was intended to look vaguely humanoid. Very suddenly, it jumped forward and kicked Justin square in the jaw, knocking the elf to his side. "Ow!"

"Justin, are you okay?" Stephen rushed to the elf, drawing Amoras and pricking his thumb on its nick. Angelo also drew his weapon, stepping towards the small rock creature.

"Yes—ow." Justin grabbed his jaw; it had already begun swelling, and was clearly bleeding inside his mouth. "I sink i's bwoken. Don' wowwy apou' me."

Angelo watched the short figure warily, waiting for it to make its move. It seemed to be doing the same of the half-elf; however, it was less patient. It ran towards Angelo, bolting between his legs and delivered a strong spin-kick to his Achilles tendon, bringing the half-elf to his knees screaming in pain. He spun around and stabbed the rock creature before it could react, pinning it to the ground through its central axis. In seconds, its limbs ceased flailing, all signs of life leaving.

"Okay, now we can worry about you. Do we have any bandages with us?" Stephen began digging through his pack frantically. "We have to tie that up so it will heal properly."

"Sthephen, I'b a wizard; I can heal it myself." He pressed his hand to his jaw and closed his eyes; a brief flash of light radiated from his palm, and he pulled it away. "It still hurts, but the bone's not broken anymore."

"And your mouth's still full of blood."

Justin spat on the ground. "Yes, I'm quite aware of that Stephen, but thank you for pointing it out anyway. Angelo, are you okay? Nothing broken?"

The half-elf shook his head. "It gave me a pretty wicked blow to the heel, but it didn't break anything. I'll just be limping for a few days, is all."

John, who had not been terribly distracted by all the conversation, looked up towards the Mountains. "Um, guys? I think they aren't done with us."

The other three looked up and saw what John was referring to—ten more little rock beings, exactly the same as the one Angelo had just ended, were approaching quite rapidly. They all swiftly rose to their feet, each drawing their weapon.

"John, how fast can you reload your crossbow?" Stephen asked of his brother.

"Fast enough; one bolt in a few seconds probably."

"Good; take out as many as you can before they reach us. Justin, please try to do the same."

"Stephen, I don't know if I can; my offensive magic isn't very good."

"None of your magic is very good Justin, but we don't have any options. Ready your offensive spells and just concentrate, please." The elf nodded and did as he was told.

"Stephen, how many do you think you can handle?" Angelo inquired, watching as John took out one in a shot.

"Maybe two at a time; my weapon is better for close range admittedly, but I've only just started using it."

"Then try to take two; I'll attempt the rest." John reloaded and fired at another, reducing it to a pile of dust. Justin concentrated and shot a bolt of lightning from his staff, stopping two more in their tracks.

The remaining six made it to the four. Stephen, as he said he would, swung and got the attention of two of them, leaving the remaining four for Angelo. The half-elf swung and was able to take out two, the other two jumping out of the way of his blade. He leaped backwards, trying to keep some distance between himself and the figures. Stephen meanwhile was enjoying quite a bit of success; he easily decapitated one, then sliced the other in half as it lunged at him.

John reloaded his crossbow one more time and fired towards Angelo, taking out another. The half-elf thrust his blade forward, but it jumped and landed on the sword unharmed. It ran up the blade, clearly making for Angelo's hand, but was stopped by another offensive spell from Justin—all ten had been defeated.

The four took the time to catch their breath after the sudden intense fight. As soon as he felt he could ask without interrupting himself for air, Stephen inquired of Justin, "So you have no idea what those were?"

Justin shook his head, "No, I do now. Those were clearly elementals. Not very strong ones though; they were probably only intended as impediments."

Angelo stood and grabbed his bag. "Well, we had probably best be on our way then; those things took quite some time to get rid of, and now that our enemy is attacking us directly, we know we're on the right track."

Justin nodded in agreement. "Indeed; this is a clear indication that our enemy hails from Feuerschloss and knows we're coming. We must make haste, lest more of those things attack us."

And so the four continued their trek towards Feuerschloss, even as the skies darkened from cloud-cover and threatened to open up on them. Indeed, they were assaulted many more times by further groups of these elemental creatures; however, with a pattern of attack recognized, they posed little more threat than slowing them down. As it became increasingly difficult to tell where they were due to the setting sun and the encroaching storm overhead, the four decided to set up camp for the night. Feuerschloss loomed overhead, a faint red glow from the depths of the volcano illuminating its outline against the stark black of its surroundings.

*   *   *

Diablo yawned, watching as the four pitched their tent at the base of the volcano. He could probably end this now if he wanted to; indeed, the group recognized this quite readily and set up a series of watches to insure such a fate did not come without some knowledge. However, he was also growing tired after the long day of sending wave after wave of ineffectual drones at these four; besides, he certainly didn't want to kill them just yet. What would the Revered think, if they decided to let them live? No, it was far better in the end, he felt, for him to attempt to get some sleep. The coming dawn would be the one wherein he would have to defend Feuerschloss, he knew; such a thing required he be well-rested.

21

Attack

The rain began to fall at dawn, awakening the four with the sudden sound of water rushing over their tarp. The sky had developed into a deep pitchblende gray with the rising sun, laced with the occasional lightning burst from deep within the cloud bank. The castle towered above them, dark as night. The fight had begun. There was no turning back now.

The four, having prepared themselves mentally for the coming conflict, stormed through the oversized front door, led by Stephen. The dark, depressing décor of the grand entry hall was like nothing they had ever seen before. Large, gothic arches spanned the height of the building itself, with a small walkway lining the wall near the ceiling to the left side. Another large door, much like the one the group had just entered, flanked the wall to their right. Several much smaller doors dotted the left wall. Straight ahead, a gigantic staircase curved around, leading to both the walkway above and an apparent basement. Everyone was overwhelmed by the size of this stunning building. What had they gotten themselves into?

"Okay," Stephen started. "John, you and Justin take the first floor rooms. Angelo, you go check out the basement. I'll look on the upper walkway."

"How will we contact each other?" asked Angelo. "This place is so large, I don't think any of us will hear each other shout." He had a point; while the entry hall echoed with their voices, it was obvious shouting would likely be useless if they were to split up in such a manner.

"We'll just have to make do with what we have," said Stephen. "We really don't have much of a choice at the moment. We have to check everywhere to ensure that whatever burned our town is properly discovered and reconciled with. If we don't split up now, what chance do we have?"

"Agreed," said John, nodding in an affirmative manner.

"Then let's go."

Stephen and Angelo ran forward together and, once they had reached the staircase, took their respective paths. This left Justin and John standing in the entry hall.

"I'll take the doors to the left," said John, "which leaves you with the large door."

"Right."

Justin ran to the right and shoved at the large door with all his might. Being made of a rather dense wood and rather large besides, it jarred just enough to let him squeeze through. After catching his breath upon such a feat of strength, he looked up to see what presence he had graced. He quickly looked down and caught his breath again.

He had entered what was clearly a great banquet hall. Before him was a table large enough for a god, made of the same wood—or at least a similar wood—as the door. How anyone could have fashioned such a furnishing was beyond his comprehension. No chair seemed to accompany it. Perhaps there was no such need, he thought. He shuddered in fear of what he might face alone. He decided a closer examination was in order.

Upon a more extensive look, Justin noticed something of which he could make little sense: a staircase had been carved into the interior of one of the table legs, and it appeared to lead up to the tabletop itself. Of course, the threat that the group wanted eliminated may very well be on top of the table, the elf realized. In spite of this possible danger, Justin started climbing.

*   *   *

Angelo plunged into the depths of the keep, ever aware that the next turn he made could be his last. He decided to check out each floor as he came to it, as after the first it was quite obvious there were several such lower chambers. If there was no need to worry about anything on that floor, he could descend further, he figured. The first door was upon him. He entered with extreme caution.

He was in what appeared to be some sort of magic laboratory. Angelo wasn't sure; he couldn't be, as he had never seen a proper one in his life (Justin's Monsoon City lab couldn't possibly count, modified as it was), but if he had, he was sure it would have looked much like this. Along the left wall was an assortment of shelves, filled with an assortment of odd items, some of which Angelo had never seen before. There were others he recognized, such as the occasional claw or horn. He didn't know the reason any of them had been kept or preserved in such a manner.

Near the center of the room was what appeared to be a cast-iron cauldron raised on a large black pillar. Next to it was a podium, on which a book rested. Upon closer inspection, Angelo recognized the writing as the same as the writing on Justin's map, the writing that Stephen had recognized runes within. Quite unlike what the half-elf expected, he felt as though he could actually read the writing this time, as though the tome had some sort of comprehension spell on it. Looking at the obvious title of the page, what had appeared to be a random assortment of lines formed letters he recognized; soon enough, the notes scribbled frantically in the margins followed, and Angelo gasped in horror at what he read. Whoever or whatever had destroyed Springsboro, they were clearly planning on destroying the rest of the world as well. Angelo, now fearing for his life, fled the room and started the next level of descent.

*　　*　　*

John knew where he was; he had seen the room countless times on his way to this place. Before him was a golden mirror, gilded with ivory sculptures of various horrific acts. *Surely these could not all have been moments in Asmodeious' life*, John reasoned. Many of the events before him he knew as having happened countless hundreds of years ago. Perhaps longevity was the reward he had been promised? He persevered on into the next room, hoping to find something to answer his own questions.

This chamber appeared to be a storage room of sorts. Boxes cluttered up along the various walls, as though someone had put them in this room to forget whatever they contained. John, though his mind told him to be inquisitive, decided that disturbing anything in this castle was probably not a good idea. As he examined the walls, he noticed no further doors, thus making this room a sort of closet; he backtracked into the main room and went into the next door.

*　　*　　*

Stephen ran up the staircase as fast as he could. This was incredibly difficult, provided the thing went most of the way up the building, and running was made more difficult by the armor the young man was wearing. He made it to the top nonetheless and, after catching his breath, decided to start at the end of the hall. In that way, he could work his way back to the staircase if need be.

He slowly opened the door, kukri at the ready. Cautiously peering in, he saw what appeared to be a very cluttered room. Books were strewn about on the floor in piles, as though the room's frequenter did not expect to need to look through the books again. It was a small, windowless room, barely ten by ten feet. In its center was a large cauldron, a shimmering silvery substance within its confines. Stephen dared not touch it; he didn't know what it was, or what it did. He instead looked at the text that happened to be lying open on the podium above the vessel. The title of the open page was "The Clairvoyance Cauldron." This intrigued Stephen, as the picture strongly resembled the object standing next to him. He quickly perused the page for any instructions on how to use it.

*   *   *

Lifting up a trap door, Justin gazed out upon the surface of the table. He pulled himself up over the edge of the hole and onto the wood. It looked somewhat smaller from the top, but Justin was not brave enough to look over the edge to see just how high he had climbed. He knew it had been quite a distance, and left it at that. He instead took notice of what was on the platform he had climbed to. Before him stood, to his surprise, another table. This one was about the right size for a large humanoid, like an average half-orc. This was an interesting piece of information, as it gave a small sense of what was being dealt with. It was very reassuring to Justin; *perhaps the large table and doors were there as intimidation*, he thought. He knew, however, that to let his guard down was to effectively kill himself. He continued searching for clues about the unknown enemy on the table.

He went over to the smaller table, where he noticed multiple dishes had piled up. *Perhaps I can find something in what this person ate.* The wizard rummaged, disgusted, through the various settings, looking for food he could identify. Looking down at the "floor," he noticed a red stain. Upon closer inspection, it became apparent to Justin that the stain was blood. He was able to identify it by scent as unicorn blood. *A weakness*, he thought. The blood of a unicorn made the one who drinks it incredibly vulnerable to a certain something, but Justin couldn't think of what it was. *If only I could remember . . .*

*   *   *

Angelo came across what appeared to be a massive library on the next floor. Shelves towered above him as he entered the room. He couldn't make out the back wall through the darkness. He ran back to the staircase, grabbed the nearest lit torch, and set off to explore.

The shelved books did not appear to have any sort of organization in their placement. Many were written in the same ancient script as the one before. *Perhaps*, he thought, *they were salvaged just before River City was laid to ruin?* Surely not, he conjectured. The one who did so would have to be several thousand years old. That didn't leave out the possibility of an ancestor of the castle dweller, but Angelo was highly doubtful. Surely nothing that old still existed.

*   *   *

John was now standing in another relatively small room; this one was not as cluttered as the storage room, but held about the same size. Not much was in this room any more, but it appeared to have once been used as a meeting room or parlor of sorts. Since that time, it had lost all of its previous glamour; only slight glimpses at such wonder existed anymore. From what he could make out, the design appeared to be of early Elven taste. Many carvings of vines and other plants were etched into the mantle of a long-forgotten fireplace. Chairs, now resting at random places throughout the room, contained very intricate details in their deteriorating cloth backings. A lamp, sitting on an end table in the center of the wall farthest from the fireplace, was easily showing its age, and looked as though it hadn't been lit since the room was last used by the previous residents. This room obviously had nothing to do with the "enemy." He took one last swift look around the room, then left.

Looking around, John saw no more doors on the left side of the entry hall. Deciding on nothing better within the scope of his assignment, he went into the large doors on the right, where Justin had been told to go before. Perhaps he was needed there. *Justin wasn't exactly the type of person who should be by himself in such a large place,* John thought. That's probably why Stephen assigned him with me. On second thought, they were the only two put together. Did Stephen really trust him all that much, to leave Justin with him? John began to have second thoughts about his mission, but they were doused as he pushed open the door and saw the contents of the dining hall.

*   *   *

Deciding that the book's instructions were accurate, Stephen deduced that it was safe to touch the liquid, and thus did so. It shimmered a little, then displayed, "Password?" Stephen hadn't counted on there being security features. How would he be able to implement the cauldron if he couldn't get past the first block? Wait . . . something was appearing in his head, why he knew not.

"Fire's Keep."

The surface of the liquid shimmered again, then allowed him access to the menu. Relieved, Stephen chose the Security option, then set the area to the castle. Immediately, several points lit up, the first showing himself. He poked at the map, around the first floor area. It next displayed John and Justin, standing on what looked to be a hardwood floor, talking to each other. The next point below was Angelo, walking through a dreary labyrinth of bookshelves, holding a torch in one hand, his sword in the other. Nothing seemed to be happening worth noting, but there were two other dots. Stephen chose to look at the one closest to him. What he saw he could not believe.

Standing out in the now drenching storm was a man in a large black overcoat. Long dark hair flowed over his broad shoulders. His back was to the screen. Before him, a spell circle had been drawn out in a red dye—blood, Stephen realized. This was their enemy; he just knew it. He had to tell the others, or at least John and Justin. Angelo probably couldn't hear Stephen from where he was. Perhaps it was better that way.

*   *   *

"Did you find anything, John?"

"Nope. How about you?"

Justin showed John all that he had found, which honestly wasn't much; it was enough, however, to gain at least a little insight into what was to come.

When Justin pointed out the bloodstain, John started to worry. A weakness in Asmodeious? Surely not; even if there was, Justin was the only one who knew how to exploit this weakness, and he couldn't remember how. *Nothing to fret over*, he told himself.

"Hey, guys!" The shout had come from the other side of the great hall. They couldn't be too sure, but it sounded like Stephen. "I've found him! He's on the roof! Come up to the second floor! The staircase to the roof is on the other side of the last room on the walkway!"

"He sounds serious," said John. "We'd better go see."

Justin agreed. This is what they had been anticipating since the beginning.

* * *

Angelo heard a faint shout in the distance. Even for a half-elf, his hearing was exquisite. He couldn't make out what was said, but he could tell that it had come from Stephen. He'd better go see what was happening, he reasoned. Perhaps there was trouble. He turned towards the door.

"Ignite."

Before him stood countless fire elementals, just like the rock ones they had encountered before. Accompanying them was a half-orc dressed in an old, ratty t-shirt and equally ratty leather pants. On his wrist was an unusually gaudy bracelet made of five stones, each a different color, set in gold. He appeared to be several years older than Angelo himself. His face, oddly enough, seemed familiar. Gray hair was tied into a ponytail in the back of his head.

"Attack!"

Crap.

The elementals lunged at Angelo with deadly accuracy. Those he couldn't dodge, he blocked with his sword. Amidst all the action, Angelo was somehow able to get his burning question out. "Who are you!?"

"My name is Diablo Villalobos. It is the name of the one who will send you to your grave!"

Oh, my. "What was your father's name?"

"I do not have a father! The man who brought me into this world, however—his name was Carlos Villalobos."

It was hard for Angelo to comprehend this sudden new revelation and still fight off elementals. He knew that his mother was not his father's first wife, but he never imagined that he was not his father's firstborn! "My name," he said amidst the confusion, "is Angelo Villalobos. *My* father was Carlos Villalobos. It's nice to meet you, half-brother."

* * *

Stephen didn't bother waiting for the others, on the off-chance that they hadn't heard him. He ran up the flight of stairs to the roof. Flinging open the doors, he shouted, "My name is Stephen Doe, and I'm here to set right what you did to Springsboro!"

The robed figure paused and turned to face the man addressing him. "I know who you are, and of your companions. I also know why you are here. Allow me to introduce myself. I am known as Asmodeious, and am the proper lord of the castle Feuerschloss. You are not going to be alive for long anyhow, so enjoy your stay as much as you can."

Stephen became consumed with rage. "How could you do such a thing as to destroy a whole town!? That's just plain evil! Have you no remorse for your actions?"

"My boy," Asmodeious spoke through a chuckle, "Springsboro was not the first city I decimated, and most certainly won't be the last. I have not felt remorse for any of my actions, and let me assure you, there are many to choose from. You do not want to get me started. On second thought, I don't want to get started. This incantation is almost done, and you will be no more."

"Not if I have anything to say about it!" screamed Stephen. He ran towards Asmodeious, who stood his ground as though nothing was going to happen.

*　　*　　*

"Never! That can't be possible! My father died at the hands of Asmodeious, which is why he couldn't save me!"

"Save you?"

Diablo pressed his face into his palm. "Asmodeious, my master, took me as a payment in a bargain my mother made with him. He told me that my father had died a pathetic wretch trying to save his only son. So you see? You can't be my half-brother!"

"Your father didn't die then—though he did die, I suspect, at the hands of this 'Asmodeious.' He went on to marry my mother."

"NO! Lies! You cannot exist!" Diablo began to conjure a magic projectile of sorts.

"I hate to do this to you upon just having met you, but I must go help my friends." Angelo jumped towards Diablo and brought the pommel of his sword down upon the half-orc's head as hard as he could. It worked; Diablo collapsed in an unconscious heap on the floor. Angelo ran up the stairs, towards where Stephen was.

* * *

John and Justin arrived on the roof to witness Stephen run across towards the robed figure. Justin had no idea who it was, but John had seen the figure all to often to not know. And now Stephen was threatening him. *This was exactly the sort of situation that would be rewarded*, he thought. Quietly, he backed up behind Justin and loaded his crossbow. He wasn't going to miss out on his reward because his brother struck first.

He was ready.

Stephen lunged at Asmodeious, and felt the most intense pain he ever had in his life spread through his chest.

Angelo thrust the doors open, just in time to watch Stephen's body hit the floor.

"What the Hell have you done!?" Angelo asked in a mixture of fury and misery. "You've killed your own brother, you monster! I knew you couldn't be trusted!"

Justin was in shock as well, if not more than Angelo. The one person who could help him, gone. What would he do now? *My life is secured as a failure now.* How could he have let this happen?

Stephen was barely alive. With his last ounce of strength, he looked up and saw something familiar: a tooth-shaped rock that had saved his life at one point. He realized he could use it to do the same now.

Asmodeious walked over to John in a nonchalant manner. "Very well done, John. As promised, here is your reward."

He held out his left hand as though in offering, then brought his fingers up to John's chin . . . and morphed his fingers into extended claws, straight through John's head.

"NO!" Another of their group had been killed swiftly. Angelo could barely take it, as his mind was still somewhat naïve.

Asmodeious retracted his hand and let John's body collapse. Pointing to him with his still-clawed hand, he said, "I never told you to kill him."

Stephen extended his arm. *Perhaps what Justin had said before was true . . .*

Angelo was in tears. "You evil, heartless, murderous son of a bitch!" He lifted his sword over his head and slashed.

Asmodeious wasn't even scratched. "Wow, you seem to have me on the money. Except, you obviously don't know one thing."

And he started to change. His right hand grew extended claws until it matched his left. The coat seemed to meld into his body. Two great, leathery wings sprouted from his back, connected at the shoulders. All this time, he was growing. His skin turned as black as the coat had been, and formed into scales all over his body. His face became elongated, and his teeth sharpened obviously. The transformation was complete, and Justin and Angelo found themselves staring into the face of a dragon, just as Diablo came running up the stairs behind them, complete with an army of elementals. With nowhere to go, it was time for them to throw down.

"Asmodeious, take control of the army. Here's the bracelet." Diablo chucked the bracelet, and Asmodeious caught it easily. "Have fun!"

"Oh, believe me, I will." He pointed to Justin and Angelo. "Keep them busy."

The miniscule marionettes started swarming the two. As they fought for their life, Asmodeious turned around and headed back to the spell circle. Only one more thing needed to be in place: his own tooth. He reached down, grabbed it, and made to put it in the center of the circle, then caught a glimpse of it. Something was wrong. He looked closer.

It had been turned into glass.

Asmodeious turned and looked down at the now dead Stephen Doe. Somehow, in his final breath, he had activated the power he had all along, and ruined Asmodeious' plan in one attempt. That was it. He wasn't going to let these remaining two off as easily as before.

"Your friend seems to have won you the battle," he said to them, "but he has assured your losing of the war!" He remembered something he had read in the spellbook before; the Elemental Summoner could be used to summon creatures of more than one element. This was the time he would test it. He walked swiftly over to the edge of the castle closest to the crater, thrust his forelimb out, and shouted, "Rock fire!"

As this was going on, Angelo had snatched John's crossbow out of his hand and, having loaded it haphazardly, aimed at Asmodeious' head. This was the first time he had ever used a ranged weapon in his life; he really hoped that he would hit his mark and that it would actually do something. He fired as Asmodeious raised his arm. The earth shook, throwing off Angelo's aim ever so slightly. The bolt missed the mark and hit the bracelet instead, shattering it into pieces and sending it into the lava pit below.

After some disgruntled snarling, Asmodeious calmed down. "No matter," he explained, "your death has already been summoned." As he said this, a gigantic bird made of magma grew out of the volcano crater. "Meet Pyror, the bird of lava. Though the bracelet was destroyed, it will still obey the one who brought it into being. I no longer have to deal with you. Pyror, destroy them as you see fit." With that, Asmodeious flew out of the way.

"Holy merciful crap." Justin was really wishing the Revered believed him and would help. There seemed no way out of this, and Pyror was bearing down on them like a literal bat out of Hell. The only thing the two of them could think of doing was to jump off the front of the castle. It would be a long drop, but they would live, as opposed to facing Pyror.

"Roll forward when you hit the ground," said Angelo. "It will soften the impact a bit, and give you a bit of forward motion to get ahead."

So they jumped the dangerous fifty or so feet, and rolled when they hit the ground. They needed all the speed they could get at this point. Especially since, as they looked back, Pyror had slammed into the ground next to Feuerschloss and was actually flowing towards them.

"Run like your life depends on it, because it does this time!" shouted Justin. He couldn't think of any way to stop an entire lava flow, unsurprisingly. So they ran as fast as they could, in the general direction of down the mountain. Not like it mattered; Pyror was a sentient being, and wasn't likely to just flow downhill. It was away from Feuerschloss, though, and thus away from the source of the lava bird's power. So they continued.

Epilogue

Justin and Angelo peered about at the new room they now found themselves in. They recognized it as the room of the Inquisition; this time however, they were able to see each other. Whatever this was, it was not meant to be an illusion.

Indeed, as the pair looked about wondering what exactly was going on, a tall figure garbed in fine golden robes approached them. She looked first at Angelo, then at Justin. "So you are the only survivors; how unfortunate."

Angelo rose and reached for his sword, only to be stopped by his companion. "Do not draw your weapon. This is Luna who stands before us, one of the Revered involved in our Inquisition. If she intended to kill us, she would have done so long ago."

The female elf nodded. "I have been watching your group since you last left this place; I'm glad I could save you when I did. The lava flow would have surely killed you otherwise."

"Lava flow!?" Angelo pushed Justin aside. "That was an elemental summon!"

Luna shook her head. "Indeed, when it began its assault it was; however, with the destruction of the summoner—that bracelet Salamandro was wearing—it ceased to be. It returned to being an ordinary lava flow."

Justin considered these words carefully, realizing just how massive the bird had been in the air. "Luna . . ." He shook his head, not wanting to contemplate the possibility.

"What you fear is true. The flow was strong and massive enough that it stretched to the very ocean." The Revered looked down and away from the two. "There was nothing I could do past saving the two of you. I apologize."

CPSIA information can be obtained
at www.ICGtesting.com
Printed in the USA
LVHW08s0138100818
586431LV00001B/26/P